A BONE TO PICK

A Peggy Henderson Adventure

A BONE
TO PICK

Gina McMurchy-Barber

DUNDURN
TORONTO

Editor: Michael Carroll
Design: Laura Boyle
Cover Design: Carmen Giraudy
Printer: Webcom

Library and Archives Canada Cataloguing in Publication

McMurchy-Barber, Gina, author
    A bone to pick / Gina McMurchy-Barber.

(A Peggy Henderson adventure)
Issued in print and electronic formats.
ISBN 978-1-4597-3072-4 (pbk.).--ISBN 978-1-4597-3073-1 (pdf).--
ISBN 978-1-4597-3074-8 (epub)

I. Title. II. Series: McMurchy-Barber, Gina. Peggy Henderson adventure.

PS8625.M86B655 2015   jC813'.6   C2015-901270-8
    C2015-901271-6

1 2 3 4 5   19   18 17 16 15

We acknowledge the support of the **Canada Council for the Arts** and the **Ontario Arts Council** for our publishing program. We also acknowledge the financial support of the **Government of Canada** through the **Canada Book Fund** and **Livres Canada Books**, and the **Government of Ontario** through the **Ontario Book Publishing Tax Credit** and the **Ontario Media Development Corporation**.

Care has been taken to trace the ownership of copyright material used in this book. The author and the publisher welcome any information enabling them to rectify any references or credits in subsequent editions.

J. Kirk Howard, President

Visit us at
Dundurn.com | @dundurnpress | Facebook.com/dundurnpress | Pinterest.com/dundurnpress

Dundurn
3 Church Street, Suite 500
Toronto, Ontario, Canada
M5E 1M2

Dedicated to Children of Integrity Montessori School

ACKNOWLEDGEMENTS

There are many people who helped me bring this book to life. I am grateful to my editor, Michael Carroll, for his respectful editing of my manuscript and for being the first to see the potential of Peggy Henderson and her archaeology adventures. I also want to thank Victoria Bartlett who — as so often in the past — asked good questions and gave useful feedback. And, finally, I want to thank three fabulous authors — Lois Peterson, Mary Ellen Reid, and Cristy Watson — for their attention to detail, lively discussions, and great cookies.

There are no ordinary moments. There is always something going on. Be present, it is the only moment that matters.

— Old Norse Saying

PROLOGUE

Sigrid learned at a very young age to be decisive in the face of danger. That is why the second her eyes fall on the great white bear she drops the driftwood and snatches the infant boy into her arms. She backs slowly toward the settlement, never taking her eyes off the giant lumbering in her direction, its nose in the air following her scent. Sigrid knows to turn and run is futile. But the determination of the hungry old bear forces her to review her plan.

As Sigrid quickly scans the barren, rolling landscape, she sees a large boulder a short distance away. It is her only option and, however slim, her only line of defence. When she reaches it, she pushes the little fellow under the slight overhang.

"Freeze, Snorri," she whispers. The child instinctively huddles against the cold rock as though it were his mother.

Sigrid slowly pulls out the long silver pin holding her cloak together and throws the garment to the ground. For an instant the pin's shiny shaft catches the light. She grips it by the intricately carved handle, and it is now a dagger in her hand. For a brief moment she thinks of her uncle's sword, the one he takes wherever he goes. What she would give to have such a weapon now! Or even her tiny fish knife would be better.

There is no time for wishful thinking. The bear is so close that Sigrid can hear its deep, heaving breaths. It must be painfully hungry, for it takes no caution and must think her an easy kill. For a brief moment she looks to the sky and pleads with the gods to give her courage to battle with this son of Aesben. Then she kisses the tiny hammer-shaped amulet hanging around her neck. It is the only thing she owns that belonged to her mother. "Thor's Mjolnir — it will protect you my dear daughter in times of danger," said Mother the day she gave it to her.

Sigrid has only one objective and only one chance — to drive the cloak pin deep into the animal's neck. In the very moment that the bear is nearly upon them, Sigrid clambers to the top of the boulder and springs onto the creature's back, letting out her fiercest Viking battle cry. In that instant she is a fearless warrior, like those in the great Norse sagas — those epic tales of gods, of their wars, of heroism, of brutality. Each story prepared her for this moment, for this life-or-death battle.

In one swift movement she raises the pin above her head and brings it down with all her might, driving it into the bear's throat. The animal lets out a frightening bellow as its blood gushes out upon its white fur. The bear rises to its hindquarters, throwing Sigrid to the ground while her pin is still lodged in the beast's throat. In a frenzy the animal whirls around. There, on the ground, is its attacker, no longer able to rise and defend herself.

The bear lifts its mighty paw and, with claws protruding like blades, sweeps up the girl's body and hurls her into the air. As she lands hard a second time, she hears her own bones crack in too many places and wails in agony.

Just as the bear is about to bring down yet another pulverizing blow onto Sigrid's small body, a hail of arrows whiz through the air and pierce, one after another, the creature's massive white body, now nearly covered with its own blood. The animal roars in anguish and staggers a short distance until it falls onto its side in a heap, groaning. Before the bear heaves its final breath, Sigrid slips into unconsciousness.

When she wakes, she no longer feels any pain. In fact, she no longer feels any part of her body at all. Has she died? she wonders. Then she hears in the distance the faint voices of the Norsemen fast approaching. It must have been their stream of arrows that finished the bear off. But then why did the arrows hail from the cover of the forest opposite the settlement? That is not her people's way. Could it have been the skraelings again?

Remembering her tiny charge, Sigrid calls out weakly to the boy. "Snorri, all is well. Come out." The little fellow crawls to her side, his small mouth puckered in fear and his cheeks stained with tears. Were she able she would comfort him in her arms, but all she can do is set her eyes intensely upon him and hold his gaze.

"Everything is all right, now. You're safe and Papa Thorfinn is coming."

The toddler sniffles and rests his tiny head on her shoulder, sucking his thumb for comfort.

Sigrid tries not to think about why her limbs do not obey her command to rise from the ground. But try as she might she cannot deny that her breathing is growing shallower with each breath.

"Should I die today will my people remember me for this deed, Snorri? Is giving my life for yours the act of a fearless Viking?" Her heart burns within, for nothing greater could she want than to be remembered as a true warrior.

Sigrid's eyes are closing, and she knows her inner light is fading. Before it is too late she sends up a prayer to Odin, the god her father worshipped.

"Oh, great Allfather, send your Valkyries to my side. Let them take me to live in Valhalla where I may sit at your feet in glory. Let not my death in battle with one of Aesben's sons be in vain." Sigrid heaves her last breath, hoping she will awake in the presence of the gods.

CHAPTER ONE

I let out an exaggerated sigh. "You know, Aunt Margaret, this brush is way too good to be used for painting the house." I ran the soft bristles over my hand and admired its perfectly formed wooden handle, while at the same time appreciating it for its greater potential.

"Too good to be used to paint? That's a pretty lame excuse for getting out of painting the house with me today. C'mon, Peggy, surely you can do better than that." Aunt Margaret pried off the lid and started stirring the turquoise paint she'd bought that morning.

"I admit it's not something I feel like doing. But I'm serious. This brush would be perfect for excavating —"

"Ha! I should have guessed — excavating indeed." Aunt Margaret snorted out a laugh — a trait of the women in my family.

"Yes, excavating," I defended, feeling annoyed.

"I thought an archaeologist needed trowels and shovels for excavating."

"They do, but once they find something really old, they have to have a tool that can gently remove the sand or dirt from the bones or artifacts that won't damage them. Imagine you found a perfectly preserved skeleton that was thousands of years old — would you want to be the one that came along and ruined it? That's why an archaeologist needs a brush like this."

Aunt Margaret snatched it from my hand. "Well, today this isn't an archaeologist's tool, but rather a paint-brush that's going to be used to give new life to our old house. And you, young lady, will have the privilege of using it." She plunged the brush into the can of paint and slapped it on the side of the house, leaving a long streak of glistening turquoise. "There, you see. It's going to be beautiful. Now get to it."

I heaved another sigh and took the now-damaged brush from my aunt. Helping her to paint the house was an idea she and Mom had cooked up as a way for me to earn my own spending money over the summer. I'd tried my best to argue that I didn't really need much spending money. After all, when you lived three blocks from the beach, all you needed was a bathing suit, a towel, and a couple of friends.

"And where will you get the money to rent a skiff at the marina when you feel like sailing?" Mom had argued. "And money for scuba diving with Vince Torino and TB? And how do you plan to pay for all those archaeology books you want to buy online?"

"Okay, I get it," I'd grumbled. My mom was a single parent, and I'd been taught young that money didn't grow on trees. I guess we were lucky — if you could call it lucky — that my mom's bossy sister and Uncle Stuart had invited us to live with them until Mom could afford to pay for a place of our own.

At first, coming to live with my aunt and uncle at Crescent Beach had been rough. But then the greatest thing in my life had happened. One summer day Uncle Stuart and I were digging a hole in the backyard for our new koi pond when we accidentally unearthed the remains of a three-thousand-year-old Coast Salish carver. That was when we first learned that Crescent Beach was actually a Coast Salish summer fishing village dating back five thousand years.

When it became clear that what at first seemed to be a large round stone was actually a human skull, everyone was in shock — well, mostly Aunt Margaret. The only thing we could think of was to call the police, who knew exactly what to do with our mystery man. They called in a provincial archaeologist, Dr. Edwina McKay. She was an expert in bones — an osteologist.

That summer Dr. McKay — or Eddy as I came to call her — taught me a lot about excavating, and how to interpret the information that ancient bones told us about a person's life and death. Besides learning a lot about the First Nations people who once lived in Crescent Beach, I also discovered I had a passion and talent for archaeology. You could say from that time on I was hooked on it.

And speaking of really old things, Eddy was one of my best friends. She got me. And thanks to her I'd been on three important excavations. My most recent was at the tip of Vancouver Island looking for a sunken fur trade ship. That was the reason why I'd gotten into scuba diving. Now, when I wasn't on some archaeological dig, I was reading and dreaming about artifacts and bones and ... well, pretty much anything to do with archaeology.

So, for obvious reasons, being drafted into painting my aunt's house felt like a prison sentence. That first day had been nothing short of agonizing — and not just because we'd spoiled a perfectly good archaeological tool. As the hot sun beat down on me, I watched jealously as tourists arrived in carloads. I knew they were all heading to Blackie's Spit where they'd park and then land themselves a spot on the beach for the day.

Then that afternoon the ice-cream man showed up and almost drove me crazy. He went by our house three times — the sound of his tinny music playing the same two bars of "Old MacDonald Had a Farm" over and over was like fingernails on a chalkboard. Each time he passed our house he slowed down as if trying to wear me down. Finally, I couldn't stand it any longer and ran after him, waving my money like a six-year-old.

By suppertime I was so tired I could hardly sit up, and holding my fork was painful. While I chewed my spaghetti and meatballs, all I could think about was how dreadful my life was going to be for the next two weeks.

"Peggy, you've worked very hard today. I'm proud of you, sweetie," Mom gushed. "Why don't you call TB and see if he'll go for a swim with you?"

"Mom," I slurred, "I'm so tired I can barely hold my eyelids open, let alone get on my bike, ride to the beach, and then swim."

"Oh, c'mon. It will be refreshing," urged Aunt Margaret. Debating with my aunt was usually a favourite pastime of mine, but I didn't even have the energy for that until she dropped a bomb on me. "By the way, I saw your friend the archaeologist at the grocery store today. She tells me she's off to work in Newfoundland — said something about Vikings."

I sat upright and nearly gagged on my meatballs. "Newfoundland — no way! Well, did Eddy say anything about me?" Funny. A moment before I was too tired to even argue with Aunt Margaret. Now I felt as if I were going to jump off my seat like a jack-in-the-box. "When's she going?" I muttered more to myself than to anyone else. "Maybe I can go, too."

Aunt Margaret snorted. "You're joking, right? Of course, you can't go —" she started saying.

"Mom, can I be excused? I have to make a call." Not waiting for her answer, I dashed out of the room. A few moments later I was punching in numbers on the phone. "Hey, Eddy, it's me."

I heard her chuckle on the other end of the line. "I was wondering how long it was going to take before I heard from you." I could feel her smile coming through the phone line. "But, Peggy, before you get your hopes up, you should know that this isn't my show. I've been asked to teach archaeology field school for Memorial University. One of their professors cancelled at the last minute, and it looks as if I was the only one who could fill in on such short notice."

"But Aunt Margaret said something about Vikings. I didn't know you were an expert on Vikings," I said, feeling my newfound energy starting to drain away.

"I'm not an expert on Vikings, but I do know about archaeology and excavating. I guess they were desperate and I was available."

"So what exactly will you be teaching?"

"These students have done a lot of classroom learning, but they've yet to go out into the field and put their theoretical knowledge into practice. They still need to learn the methods of excavating a site — surveying, mapping, setting datum points, using tools properly ..."

"In other words, things I already know how to do."

Eddy chuckled again. "Believe it or not, Peggy, you still have much to learn."

"Maybe so, but I bet I know more than the students you'll be teaching at field school."

"Well, you could be right."

"So I still don't get what the Vikings have to do with field school."

"Right, well this year Memorial's field school is at a place at the northern tip of Newfoundland called L'Anse aux Meadows. A while back a couple of archaeologists discovered some Viking artifacts there. After eight years of excavating, they proved it's an authentic Norse site — in fact, it's the only one in North America," explained Eddy. I remembered learning a bit about the Vikings in school. Like how they came to the East Coast of Canada a thousand years ago. "It turned out to be so important that the place is now a UNESCO World Heritage Site."

"Is that the organization that protects special places and things?" I asked Eddy.

"That's right, although they do a lot more than that." There was a moment of silence over the line. "So, anyway, L'Anse aux Meadows is where this year's field school is going to take place. And I'm really excited because I haven't been there in nearly twenty years."

Hmm. I needed a few moments to think this through. I was practically Eddy's sidekick — like Robin was to Batman or Tonto to the Lone Ranger. If Eddy was going to Newfoundland to teach a bunch of greenhorns how to excavate, there had to be something I could do to help.

"I know what's going through your head, Peggy. Believe me, if there was something I could do, I would. But these students are serious about having a career in archaeology and have paid a lot of money to attend this special summer course. I don't think they'd be happy about having a thirteen-year-old girl — as experienced and knowledgeable as she may be — teach them about excavating."

"Okay, then, sign me up. I'll go as a student."

"If, and I am saying *if* you could sign up as a student, just where would you get the $2,500 for tuition and living expenses, plus $1,000 for airfare?"

My jaw fell, and I sighed. "Oh, right." Even with all the money I had in my savings and the money I would get paid to paint the house, I'd have nowhere near enough.

"I'm sorry. If something changes, you'll be the first to know," said Eddy.

By the time I hung up, the overwhelming tiredness I'd felt at dinner had returned.

That night, as I lay in bed disappointed and sleepy, Mom popped into my room to say good night.

"It would have been wonderful if you could have gone, Peggy," Mom said. "But if going to Newfoundland to excavate a Viking site isn't in the cards, then something equally wonderful is right around the corner. You'll see."

"Mom, I appreciate that you want to cheer me up, but I seriously doubt there'd be anything as cool as going with Eddy to see where the Vikings lived." I pulled the blanket over my head.

As unlikely as it was, I went to sleep that night hoping Eddy would find a way to take me. After all, miracles did happen, right?

"Here's a thought — how about I go out and get started on painting while you stay here and make the chili for dinner?" Aunt Margaret suggested cheerfully after Mom left for work the next morning.

Now it was my turn to snort out a laugh. "Right, me make dinner? You know I have a hard time boiling water without burning it."

"Oh, come on, Peggy. Anyone can cook. You've done it before. You just have to follow the recipe." I watched her load measuring cups, cans of tomatoes and beans, spices, and a bunch of other stuff onto the counter. "Here's the recipe — just follow it exactly and you can't fail." She handed me the piece of paper, which read: BEST CHILI CON CARNE ON EARTH.

I decided being left to make chili was probably better than standing in the heat slopping paint on the house and on myself. I skimmed through the recipe — it said something about browning meat and onions first. Now to me that just didn't make sense. Why cook the meat and onions first when they were just going to have to go into another pot to cook again? Instead, I took a shortcut and threw all the ingredients into one big pot and turned up the stove good and high so it would cook faster. Why have chili for dinner when we could have it for lunch? Doing things my way saved not only time, but also meant one less frying pan to wash up. Satisfied that maybe I was better at cooking than I gave myself credit for, I strolled outside.

"You're finished already?"

I shrugged. "Sure."

"You followed the recipe, right?" Aunt Margaret asked.

"Don't be so suspicious. I followed it more or less."

She narrowed her eyes. "More or less? That's Great-Aunt Beatrix's recipe, and if it's done right, it really is the greatest chili on earth."

"Don't worry, Aunt Margaret. You'll see — it'll be fine. And I'll bet even GAB would be happy."

"GAB … what's that?"

"Really? GAB — Great-Aunt Beatrix, of course!"

Aunt Margaret rolled her eyes at me.

For the next hour I painted windowsills and doors with glossy white paint. I had to admit my mind wasn't on the job and there was nearly as much paint on the grass and sidewalk as on the house. All I could think about was how much I wanted to go with Eddy to Newfoundland. It was nearly noon when the phone rang and Aunt Margaret ran to get it.

A few minutes later I had a horrible thought. What if the caller was Eddy? What if she figured out a way for me to go? Would Aunt Margaret tell me about it? Or would she tell Eddy I was too busy to go because I had to stay and help her paint? I wasn't going to take a chance on it and dashed into the kitchen. When I opened the door, a thick, hazy swirl seeped out of the kitchen and smelled like burnt tires. As I stepped inside, Aunt Margaret was throwing open the windows and fanning the air.

"Who was on the phone?" I asked casually.

"Are you kidding me? Who cares about the phone? Peggy, can't you see what's happened — the chili boiled over and was burning on the stove element! With the amount of fat on the surface we're just lucky it didn't start a fire."

That was when I noticed the stove and floor for the first time. It seemed as if a volcano had erupted. "Sorry about that. I guess I turned it on a little too high." She handed me the paper towel and I started to wipe up the floor. "So, anyway, did you catch who was on the phone?" I asked again. Aunt Margaret growled, and I knew if I looked her in the eye I'd see she was giving me one of her one-eyed glares.

"You not only turned it on too high but clearly you either didn't cook the meat first or you failed to drain off the fat." She threw me a wet washcloth. "And as for who was on the phone, I didn't get a chance to answer, but I'm grateful he or she was calling. Otherwise we could be fighting a fire right now." She dragged out the mop and bucket and began filling it with water. "Really, Peggy, were you just trying to prove you really are a bad cook so I'd never ask you again?"

"Harsh, Aunt Margaret," I shot back.

"Well, you're going to have to learn to cook better sooner or later unless you plan on eating toast and cereal your whole life," she said.

I didn't respond. As far as I was concerned, living off toast and cereal didn't sound too bad to me. Besides, learning to cook better wasn't necessary when you could just open a package or hit the drive-through.

For the rest of the day, every time the phone rang I nearly went berserk, hoping it was Eddy calling to give me some good news. But each time it wasn't her I plunged deeper into despair, seeing days and weeks ahead of me, spent slapping paint onto my aunt's old house. As far as I was concerned, there was only one good reason to have a paintbrush in hand — and that was for brushing away sand and dirt from an ancient artifact or burial.

Then, just when I thought I was as low as I could get, Eddy called. When Aunt Margaret handed me the phone, my knees were shaking.

"Hi, Eddy. I was hoping I'd hear from you. Got some good news for me?" Her silence made me feel like a balloon with a tiny hole, and I was slowly deflating.

"Hi, Peggy. I'm leaving about five tomorrow morning. Probably won't get to L'Anse aux Meadows until late evening. I just wanted to say goodbye …" Silence again. "I really did try every angle and there's just nothing I can do. I'm afraid you'll have to sit this one out."

I sank onto the chair as the news settled in my mind. "That's okay," I said in my best pretend-cheerful voice. "Have a good trip, and I'll see you when you get back."

"Is there anything I can bring you?" Eddy asked.

Pushing my disappointment aside, I tried to think of something. "How about one of those cheesy Viking helmets with the horns? That would be kind of classic."

"Sure thing. I bet some gift shop there will have them. Although you should know that horns on Viking helmets are all fiction and Hollywood."

"No horns on their helmets? Geez, another blow." After that I could tell the conversation was getting awkward, so I wished Eddy a good trip and hung up.

"Well, I'm glad that's all over with," came a voice from behind me. I quickly turned to see Aunt Margaret standing in the doorway. I'd forgotten she was there. "Now maybe you'll get focused on other things — like getting more paint on the house and less on the grass. And if you're good, I'll teach you how to make chili the right way."

"Oh, goodie gumdrops, I can hardly wait." I clapped my hands as if I were three.

Aunt Margaret shook her head and gave me a look that said, *Peggy, you're such a weird kid.*

CHAPTER TWO

"Thanks for letting me go with you," TB said to my mom as she backed the car out of the driveway.

"We're delighted you could join us, Thorbert. It isn't every day we get to take in a Viking exhibit with a real-life Viking." It was awful watching TB's face turning eight shades of red.

"Well, actually, Mrs. Henderson, I'm only Norse on my father's side. I don't know if any of my ancestors were actually Vikings."

"Vikings, Norse … weren't they all the same?" Mom asked as we sped down the highway toward the ferry that would take us to Vancouver Island.

"Actually, most Norse people were farmers, fishermen, or traders," TB said. "However, sometimes they went on a Viking. A Viking was often a trading expedition, but, yes, there were times when they turned into raids that may have involved a few gory murders and plundering of villages. But in general the Norsemen probably were no worse than other warring tribes of that time."

"Well, there you go, I've already learned something new, and we haven't even gotten to the museum," Mom said.

Going to the Royal British Columbia Museum in Victoria to see the Viking exhibit was Mom's way of helping me to cheer up after she'd heard about Eddy's phone call. At first I wasn't all that interested in going. I am one of those people who would rather play the game than watch it. As far as I was concerned, going to see a bunch of ancient artifacts in glass cases wasn't nearly as much fun as being the one to actually dig them up. When I mentioned the exhibit to TB, he nearly fell to the ground and begged me to ask my mom if he could go, too. His parents were always too busy to take him to stuff like that. And ever since he'd seen the ad on TV about the exhibit coming to town, he wanted to go. How could I refuse?

When we got to the museum, there was a huge lineup waiting to get in. I didn't realize the Vikings fascinated so many people. TB was like a little kid, hopping around until we got inside. After that I hardly saw him, well, except when he came back every ten minutes so he could drag me off to see something he found exciting. "C'mon, Peggy, you've got to see this," he demanded, not letting up until I followed him. While he was pretty annoying, I admit his excitement was infectious.

"Take a look at this sword," TB said. It was only a replica of a real Viking sword, but the handle was decorated with beautiful engravings and there was a large red ruby embedded on both sides. "You're allowed to pick it up, Peggy. Try it."

I gripped the handle and lifted the sword. It was solid and heavy, and the blade reflected the light. I tried wielding it, but could tell that it would take a lot of strength and skill to control it.

"You could sure do a lot of damage with a thing like that," TB said admiringly.

"Yup, it's a real Slice-O-Matic … slices, dices, and chops up anything. Probably not so good for cutting bread," I said.

"Yah, and it wouldn't fit in the knife drawer very well," Mom added when she came up from behind.

"True, Mom. So true."

As I made my way around the exhibit, I learned stuff like it wasn't just men who went on a Viking trip — sometimes women and teens could go, too. Then minutes after I'd read the plaque that said Vikings didn't have horned helmets — some old composer named Richard Wagner got that started — TB tapped me on the shoulder.

"Hey, look at me," he said, smiling proudly. He was wearing a Viking helmet — and, yup, it had horns.

"Obviously, you've been to the gift shop," I said. "Maybe you should have read this sign before buying that."

He looked down at the sign and shrugged. "That's Hollywood for you! Hey, Peggy, I just heard a great joke. One time Thor decided to go down to Earth and introduce himself to a beautiful lady who was standing at a bus stop." TB snickered. "He said to the lady in a deep, booming voice, 'I'm Thor.' The lady turned to him and said, 'You're thor? Oh, my god, my feet are so thor I can hardly wait to thit.'" TB buckled over with laughter as if it was the funniest thing ever. "What? Don't you get it? The lady had a lisp — thor, sore, thit, sit? Oh, never mind — you're a joke killer."

After that TB slipped off to learn about Viking ships. I didn't bother because he kept dashing back and forth to give me the rundown. "Their ships were flat so they could go up shallow rivers — kind of handy for raiding villages, right?" Then a few minutes later, "I just read they were the first to build ships that could sail the ocean and carry large cargo. Handy, right?"

For me the best part was the stuff on burials.

"Ew," sneered TB as I peered into a glass case with the dried-up bones of some dead guy. "Figures you'd be interested in this stuff."

"Get used to it, TB. Dead people are my thing." The Vikings had two kinds of burials. Inhumation — that was pretty basic, really, burying the dead in the ground. And the other was cremation. Some Vikings believed if they cremated the dead person his soul was freed to begin life in the next realm.

"It says here sometimes they cremated important people in ships. How crazy is that? To burn a perfectly useful boat," complained TB.

"That's crazy, but not as bad as putting in fifty years to build a stone pyramid for some dead Egyptian king and his stuff," I added.

On the ferry ride home we sat on the observation deck where we could see the sky all pink and orange and watch the seagulls ride the wind. When the sun sank below the horizon, TB got all focused on some Viking game he'd downloaded on his phone from the museum app store. After that he didn't make a peep.

"Thanks, Mom," I said contentedly. "That was a great day — better than I imagined."

She beamed at me and passed me a gift bag. "I'm glad you enjoyed yourself, Peggy. This is just a little souvenir of our day together."

I opened the bag and pulled out a beautiful book called *Ancient Norse Sagas*. "This is great. Thanks."

I looked at my watch. It was just after nine. Newfoundland was four and a half hours ahead, which meant Eddy had arrived. She was probably tucked in bed by now and ready to start field school in the morning.

"Thinking about Eddy?" Mom asked.

I nodded.

"Well, never mind, sweetheart, there will be lots of wonderful adventures ahead for you, too."

Maybe, but none would be as cool as going to the only site in North America that was an actual Viking outpost.

By the time my head hit the pillow that night, I was zonked to the nth degree. Aunt Margaret had agreed to let me sleep in the next morning after I promised I'd put in at least four hours of painting later in the afternoon. As tired as I was, I opened my book of Viking stories and sleepily leafed through the pages. There were "The King's Sagas," "The Hero Sagas," "Sagas of the Viking Gods," and "The Creation of the World Saga." That seemed like a good place to start.

> Long ago, out of the damp mist and darkness of Niflheim and the burning fire of Muspellheim, came great spires of hoarfrost, mountainous blocks of ice, and brilliant sparks that filled the valleys of Ginnungagap. Soon after there arose from this massive wonder the very first giant, Ymir, and Audumla, the

cow. Ymir drank milk from Audumla's udder, and it gave him great strength. At the same time Audumla, the cow, licked the blocks of salty ice for her nourishment. And as she licked and licked, out of the salty ice came Buri. He was the first of the gods. He was tall and handsome and in time became the father of all creatures. Through magic he had a son named Borr who married Bestla, a friendly and good giant. This couple gave birth to three sons, Odin, Vili, and Ve. But Odin was the strongest of the three and was more powerful than his father and brothers.

In time Ymir fathered more giants. They were evil beings and were more in number than the goodly gods. But they had not the power to prevail over them. Then one day the three young brothers knew they must hunt down and kill Ymir if there was ever to be peace. It was not such a difficult task for them, and from his remains they in turn created the world.

They transformed Ymir's blood into oceans and fresh water, his flesh became the land, his bones turned into mountains, his teeth the rocks, and his hair became the grass and trees. They saved his eyelashes to make Midgard — Middle Earth — the place where humans would dwell. Then they threw Ymir's head into the air, and his brain became the clouds and his skull the sky.

Next the three brothers grabbed some of the sparks shooting out from Muspellheim, the land of fire. They threw them up into the sky where they turned into twinkling stars. Afterward the brothers built Asgard, which became the sacred home of the gods.

I was way too sleepy to read more and closed the book. I hoped the image of brains exploding into stars didn't turn into a nightmare. Just as I was drifting off to sleep, somewhere far away in the land of the awake, I heard my mom's phone ring. It was unusual for someone to call so late, but I didn't have the strength or interest to give it much thought. I simply let my head melt into the pillow, and I slipped off to what I thought was going to be a good long sleep.

The house is lit by the glow of the fire. Everyone sits around as Thorfinn readies for the telling of the evening story. The men sharpen their knives and polish swords. The boys practise their carving and the girls their sewing and weaving. The mothers tend to the babies or clean up from the evening meal.

"Someone remind me — where did I leave off?" Thorfinn asks.

"Last night you told the story about the creation of the gods and Asgard," Sigrid says.

"Ah, that's right. You were paying attention." Thorfinn smiles at his young charge. He is a big man, red-bearded, and is inclined to be of good temper. His young charge loves him as a father. And though she has heard the story of creation many times in her life, each time is as good as the first.

"I always pay attention when you're telling the stories, Uncle. I listen better than anyone else."

Thorfinn laughs deeply at the girl's declaration. What he does not know is that she is memorizing the stories so that one day she can be their keeper and tell them to the others.

Ever since she was very little, even before her parents perished in the house fire, Sigrid loved listening to the stories the elders tell at the end of the day when the clan comes together for supper. Some stories are of the gods and goddesses. Other stories are of great explorers, like Erik the Red and his son, Lucky Leif, the first to come to Vinland, the cold and windy settlement they now occupy. But Sigrid enjoys most the stories with shield maidens, those brave and clever women who preferred to take up the sword and fight in battle than live out their lives cooking and cleaning and raising children. When she is old enough, she, too, will be a shield maiden — if her guardians let her.

"All right, then let us continue. When the gods were finished creating Asgard, they took time to rest and enjoy their work. But there was a giant, Hrimthurs, who wagered the gods that he could build a wall around Asgard in one winter. If he succeeded, then they must give him the sun and the moon, and the lovely Frigga for a wife. Now Loki, adopted son of Odin, had little faith in Hrimthurs, so he convinced Odin, Thor, and the other gods to accept the *wager. Upon this agreement the giant began his work with the help of his giant horse, Svadilfari."*

As Thorfinn recites the well-worn story, Sigrid sits on the edge of her seat, biting her nails. She sees in her imagination the giant, an ugly brute who thinks he can outsmart the gods and take for himself the beautiful Frigga. He must be mad, she thinks. He deserves the gory mess he will soon be in for daring to outwit Odin and the others.

"Sigrid, please take Snorri and tuck him into bed," asks Gudrid. "He's very tired tonight."

"Now? We're in the middle of a story. He can wait till later," Sigrid snaps back. Just then the toddler lets out an ear-splitting wail that commands attention.

"I go sleep now," he cries.

"Sigrid, do as you were told," Thorfinn commands.

The girl huffs and grabs the little fellow by the hand. "Come on," she says as she yanks him from his mother's lap. "Brat," she says when they are out of earshot. As Sigrid tucks the toddler under the fur blanket, his eyes are already closed and his thumb is in his mouth. "Why do I always get stuck with you? I'm not your mother. And for that matter I'll never be anyone's mother. I'm going to be a shield maiden."

Sigrid knows if anyone heard her say such a thing — anyone except Snorri — they would laugh at her. No woman in her clan has ever become a warrior, let alone an orphan girl like her. But at the core of her being she knows she has the heart of a warrior, like Thor, and that is more important than anything.

The girl lays her head down beside her cousin and whispers in his ear, "One day, Snorri, you'll see. I will *march into battle and strike down the enemy as fiercely as if I were Odin, the Allfather himself. They will call me Sigrid the Brave. You'll see ..." With images of fighting giants and dwarfs single-handed, she slips off to sleep.*

CHAPTER THREE

The next morning came way too soon. Before the sun was fully up, Mom was in my room rattling around in my closet. Out of one eye I watched her open and shut drawers and pull my suitcase out from under my bed.

"Mom," I growled, "what are you doing? I'm trying to sleep here!" She either didn't hear me or didn't care because she kept on thumping around. I pulled my pillow over my head. "This isn't fair. Aunt Margaret said I could sleep in."

"Never mind. You can sleep on the plane," she said.

I lifted my head slightly and watched her shove my clothes into the suitcase.

"Okay, that should be enough shirts and pants, undies and warm sweaters. Oh, where's your raincoat? I've looked everywhere for it."

I sat up and stared at her. "Have you finally lost your marbles? What are you talking about?" I asked, now completely annoyed. "It's a perfectly sunny summer day. Why would I need my raincoat? Mom, stop. Why are you packing my suitcase?"

Mom just beamed at me, then looked at her watch. "We don't have much time for this, but here's the short version. Last night Eddy called." I sat up quickly and could feel my heart pounding under my pajamas. "As it turns out, the field school is in need of a cook's assistant.

Apparently, they had someone lined up, but after just one day he suddenly quit. Eddy said that as soon as she heard she thought of you."

I didn't say anything, just stared at her.

"Peggy! You're going to Newfoundland!"

"What? But …" My brain was shorting out. "Cook's assistant? I'm a terrible cook."

"Anyone can cook. And besides, you made that wonderful chili for dinner the other night." What Mom didn't know was that Aunt Margaret salvaged what she could from the chili I'd burned and prepared the rest.

"Seriously, Mom, I can't really cook. And even if I could, why would I want to go all the way to L'Anse aux Meadows just to get stuck cooking while everyone else was out excavating?"

"Look, Peggy, when you get offered a free trip —"

"Free trip?"

"That's right. Eddy said the field school is willing to pay for your airfare and give you free room and board in exchange for being the cook's help. The catch is that you have to leave today and be willing to start tomorrow morning." I frowned. "Oh, and she did warn that the cook is pretty overbearing, but I figured that she can't be much worse than your Aunt Margaret."

I sat on the edge of my bed, hugging my pillow, not quite sure what to make of it all.

"Peggy, think about it. You're not going to be cooking all day and all night. This is your big chance to actually see the place where the Vikings explored and lived … not just look at some artifacts in a museum case. And who knows, maybe you'll be able to excavate with the students in your spare time. Peggy, it's a chance of a life-time and is full of potential!"

Though I still felt like a deer in headlights, I was finally starting to get the picture.

"Now get up, girl. Everything's been arranged. I booked your plane online and it leaves at nine, but we have to be at the airport no later than seven-thirty."

A half hour later I'd showered, finished packing, and was standing at the front door, waiting for Mom who was frantically trying to find the keys to the car. Aunt Margaret sat on the stairs, frowning.

"This is crazy, Lizzy. What mother packs her daughter off to Newfoundland on a moment's notice? You haven't thought this thing through. And, besides, what does Peggy know about being a cook's helper?" She looked at me when she said that.

"I know, that's what I said, too," I agreed sheepishly. "But I do know how to peel potatoes and carrots. And, besides, you're the one who said cooking's easy."

"Found them," Mom said, rattling her keys as she dashed down the hall toward me and the door. "Sorry, Margie. I don't have time to argue about this again. As I said, they were looking for someone who could go immediately. This is Peggy's big chance. I had to take it." She kissed Aunt Margaret and pushed me and my suit-case out the door. "C'mon, c'mon, we've got to get going."

"Wait," insisted Aunt Margaret. A moment later she came out to the car and handed me a book, *Cooking Made Easy for Kids*, along with a toque and mittens. "After your experience in the kitchen the other day, I got this cookbook as a little surprise."

Oh, wonderful, I thought, *just the kind of surprise every kid likes to get!*

"Now that you won't be around, you might as well take it. Might come in handy."

I seriously doubted it, but did my best to give her my out-of-this-world happy look.

"You don't fool me. I know you'd be happier if it was some book about bones or arrowheads. Anyway, basically it's true, cooking is easy — *if* you follow the recipes. I stuck in GAB's best chili in the world recipe, too. Don't lose it!"

"GAB?" Mom questioned.

"GAB ... short for Great-Aunt Beatrix," I explained. Suddenly, all three of us were snort-laughing our heads off like a pack of piglets. When we finally pulled ourselves together, I asked, "What's with the hat and mitts?"

"You're going to Newfoundland, Peggy," Aunt Margaret said.

I was about to remind her that it was summer when she put her hand over my mouth.

"Trust me on this one. If it's overcast and windy, even summer in Newfoundland can feel cold. There will be days when you'll be glad you have them." Then Aunt Margaret shoved them into my carry-on case, and I thought for once it was best not to argue.

As we drove to Vancouver International Airport, Mom gave me my flight itinerary and all the instructions I needed to get to Deer Lake, Newfoundland, where someone from the field school was meeting me.

"I know it might look overwhelming, but you'll be in the care of airline staff the whole time. They do that for underage travellers flying on their own," explained Mom.

I'd only been on a plane once before and that was with Mom when we went to Edmonton for my cousin Ava's wedding. "So you're flying to Toronto and then have a one-hour layover. From there you'll fly to Deer Lake."

I did the math on my fingers. A four-hour flight to Toronto, plus a one-hour layover, plus a three-hour flight to Deer Lake. "That's not so bad. I'll be there before suppertime."

"Ah, well, actually more like bedtime — a very late bedtime. Don't forget, there's a four-and-a-half-hour time change, and, well … there's a bit of a drive from the airport to the field camp."

"A bit of a drive … like what, an hour?"

"More like five hours," she said, wincing.

"What? No way! Five hours. That means I won't get there until way after midnight!" I could already feel my sore butt.

After lots of hugs and kisses, Mom passed me over to a flight attendant who promised I would be in safe hands. I was lucky to get a window seat. During the flight, I spent most of the time with my nose pressed against the window, watching the Canadian landscape change from mountains to rolling hills to fields of wheat to what looked like an ocean but was really Lake Superior. I followed our flight path on the screen in front of me, too.

When I boarded the small jet in Toronto that would fly me to Newfoundland, I was surprised to see there were only about twenty other people on the flight. I was equally surprised when we arrived at the Deer Lake airport. Within minutes of landing, the plane was empty and the other passengers had disappeared faster than ice cream on a hot day.

I stood outside the terminal, waiting for my ride. Mom said someone named Robbie was coming for me. She didn't know if Robbie was a girl or a guy or what kind of vehicle to look for. But the moment I heard rattling and then saw a smoking Datsun come billowing through the gates I had a feeling I would soon find out.

"Hey, are you Peggy?" asked a girl wearing a Viking helmet with horns and tattoos all down her arms. "'Cause if you are, I'm Robbie and I'm here to get you."

I remembered what Mom had said about the ride to L'Anse aux Meadows being five hours long and wondered if Robbie's old beater would really get us there. "Yes, I'm Peggy."

"Great. Well, come on, kid. We'll grab some burgers from McMoodles down the road and then get going. If we don't run down a deer or moose, then there's a good chance we'll be at field camp by two-thirty or so in the morning, but lights will be out 'cause they shut off the generator at ten-thirty." While I was trying to get a sideways look at Robbie's tattoos, she was studying me, too. "It's kinda unusual for a kid to want to come all the way across the country like this. You like cooking, do you? Are you some kind of Martha Stewart wannabe?"

"Martha who? Is that the cook's name?"

Robbie snickered at my question. "No, Bertha is camp cook. She's a fantastic cook, too — just a little rough around the edges, if you know what I mean."

I wasn't sure I did know what she meant, but I wasn't planning to be around much, anyway. I figured I'd put in an hour or two stirring soup, peeling potatoes, or serving up food, then I'd take off to see if I could get in on

42

the excavation part of field school. It was perfect, really. I'd miss all the boring lectures and go straight over to the dig. That was where I'd show those university students I wasn't really a cook's help, but an experienced archaeologist — well, amateur archaeologist.

We rattled down Viking Trail Highway. When I glanced in the side rearview mirror, I saw white clouds puffing out our rear end like smoke signals. And after the first fifty kilometres, Robbie was more interested in singing than talking.

"You like Guns N' Roses?" she shouted over the music blasting from the speakers. "This is my favourite number — 'Dust N' Bones.'"

I didn't know Robbie well enough to tell her that her rowdy old-school rock music was giving me a headache. But after three albums of it I finally stuck my fingers in my ears and tried to focus on the scenery — what I could see of it in the gloom.

A few hours later we stopped for gas in a place called Gunners Cove. Out on the water, floating mountains of ice glistened in the moonlight. I'd seen pictures of icebergs but never knew just how powerful and huge they were in real life.

"Somethin', eh?" Robbie said when we got back into the car. "Some people call this coastline Iceberg Alley."

"Yah, I knew that. I also know that 90 percent of an iceberg's mass is actually below the water."

"Sure. But I bet you didn't know that icebergs aren't salty —"

"Of course, they aren't salty. They're glaciers and were formed from snow," I said. She looked annoyed, maybe because I was smarter than she thought. "I also know that the Vikings reached North America five hundred years before Columbus and that they never wore horned helmets."

Robbie gave a nasty smile and knocked her helmet with her fist. "You're kind of a little know-it-all, eh?"

My cheeks suddenly burned. "What? I was only sharing information I got from Eddy, geez."

"Of course, I knew Vikings didn't have horned helmets. It just so happens I love touristy junk and couldn't resist owning one of these puppies — all part of the fun of being at Viking field school. So who's Eddy? Your boyfriend?"

I snorted. "My boyfriend? No! Eddy's one of the field school instructors."

"Are you talking about Dr. McKay? You know her?"

"Know her? I'm like her assistant. Everything I know about archaeology — which is considerable — I learned from her. In fact, I've been on several important real-life excavations and —"

"Yay! We're finally here," Robbie interrupted. "Phew. Don't think I could have handled another minute. It sure was getting stuffy in here." She looked at me and fanned herself.

There were no lights — even the moon had vanished — so the night sky was inky black as we drove up to the meadows. While I couldn't see the ocean, I did hear the waves lapping on the shore in the distance. After we parked, Robbie took out a flashlight and shone it in my eyes. "Like I warned you, lights go out by ten-thirty. C'mon, I'll show you where you'll be bunking."

Robbie pulled out my bag from the trunk of the car and dragged it to the nearest tent. "You'll want to be real quiet," she whispered. "From the sound of it, Bertha is asleep. And trust me, you don't want to wake her up."

"What? I'm supposed to sleep in a tent with someone I've never even met?" I whispered back. "Maybe we should find Eddy —"

"Shh! Those are the orders, kid. Straight from Professor Brant. He's the chief around here, and you do what he says if you want things to go well." Robbie shone the flashlight across the tent. "That's your cot over there. Probably best to just crawl in and get some sleep while you can. You've got an early start in the morning." After I'd stumbled to my bed, Robbie waved and then whispered, "Good luck."

I heard her giggling on her way out. Good luck? Why would I need good luck?

An hour later, still not able to fall asleep, I figured out why. Bertha snored like a hound dog with a head cold. And if that wasn't bad enough, she burped and then there was the thunder coming from under her blanket. Soon after, the air in the tent was toxic, too. She was some kind of noise machine: *Snuzzz, blurp, craccck, snuzzz, blurp, craccck.* If there was a way out, I would have taken it, but it was too dark. And besides, if this was how noisy she could be in her sleep, what would she be like if I woke her?

Sometime after three in the morning I must have been so tired that even the human generator next to me couldn't keep me awake.

"Sigrid Thorbjornsdottir, put down your uncle's sword and get back to your work," scolds Gudrid. "When you're finished with gutting and cleaning the fish for our evening

meal, I need you to come and watch Snorri while I help Thorfinn in the wood shop."

Sigrid struggles to raise the heavy sword and waves it in the air just once before setting it down by Thorfinn's chair. She admires the way the firelight glints off its shiny blade, and imagines how many times it has been used to strike down an enemy.

"Come now, my dear, you need to get your mind straight. How many times have I told you that each of us was made to fulfill a certain role? You, my girl, are not a warrior, no matter how brave you may be."

"That's ridiculous, Aunt Gudrid, and a waste. I'm every bit as strong, fierce, and capable as any boy — and much more clever."

Her aunt smiles and draws the girl in for an embrace. "Maybe so, Sigrid, my dear. But the goddess Frigga has determined that you shall be a wife on your next birthday and with her blessing a mother soon after that. Now get on with your work like a good girl."

Sigrid curses the goddess Frigga for her blunder in creating her a girl instead of a boy. She kicks at the dirt and throws on her cloak. As she bends over to take up the string of fish, she snags her woollen tunic on the corner of the hearth and tears it.

"Stupid thing," she curses. "And which of the gods divined that girls should wear such awkward things. Girls should be allowed to wear trousers like the boys."

Gudrid laughs good-naturedly. "Such a temper, girl, such a temper. No man is going to want a wife like that."

"Good, because I don't want a husband — not now, and not when I turn thirteen, not ever." Sigrid thinks of the wrinkled old trader, Bjorni, who asked Uncle Thorfinn to let him have her hand in marriage when they return to Greenland. He is rich and well settled. But surely her uncle would not agree to the union.

Out in the brisk air, Sigrid feels as dark and cold as the lowering clouds threatening to pour down on her. She pulls her thin cloak close about her and walks through the camp toward the stream. On her way she hears the usual sounds of people at work — clanging of metal on metal coming from the forge, the hammer driving in nails in the wood shop next door, and so many other voices. Some of them from the women sitting outside the workshop on stools, chatting as they deftly sew up breaks in the fish netting.

Sigrid sighs. She is afraid Gudrid is right about everyone having one destiny and purpose, and that hers is merely to be a wife and mother. She kicks at the stones along the path and wonders why she could not be like Stikla, the warrior girl who ran away from home, preferring the life of war over marriage. Maybe that is what she should do — run away.

"I know what you're thinking, but those maiden warriors were not just common girls. Gautrekssonar, she was the only child of King Eirikr. Unlike you, she was of royal blood," said Aunt Gudrid some time ago. She said it not to make Sigrid feel bad, but only to state a simple fact. It is true. Sigrid is not of noble lineage. But she cannot help being this way. She did not plan to be the kind of girl who would rather wield a sword than sew or cook. It is just the way she is.

Sigrid follows the trail to the narrow stream. She drops the fish into the water to clean them. Soon they will become another boiled fish stew. She is tired of fish stew and hopes the men will go out hunting soon for fresh deer meat. She would not even mind a few scrawny squirrels or hares, though they are much more work to prepare. If her uncle would let her, she would gladly go and get some herself since she has mastered the bow and loves to hunt.

As she draws out her gutting knife, Sigrid slowly turns the small dagger-like blade from side to side. It is sharp and pointy. It could inflict pain and damage should the need arise. She whirls around and stabs violently into the air, imagining she is suddenly faced with a force of dark elves and fire giants.

"Ha!" she shouts as she brings down the first of the giants. Then she turns to the right and slashes out again with her would-be dagger. "Take that, you wretched elves. Come out into the sun and turn to stone." Suddenly, Sigrid is aware of being watched. When she turns around, there is her cousin, Gunnar, smirking at her.

"Oh, Sigrid the brave, save me, save me," he squeals in a mocking voice. "Please do not let the ugly ogre eat me." He buckles over with laughter.

In a flash Sigrid drops her knife, dashes over, and rams his head under her arm, squeezing until he shrieks in pain and asks for mercy. She pushes him to the ground and stands over him. "Remember the parable — brawl with a pig and you go away smelling like a pig? I might never become a warrior, but I take pleasure knowing that neither will you."

The lad gets off the ground and rubs his neck. "You're mean, cousin." The boy glares at Sigrid while brushing off his tunic. "You could learn to laugh more." Gunnar turns and walks back toward the camp. "By the way, I *was coming to help you clean the fish, but I think I'll find some other work to do instead."*

Sigrid's cheeks burn now. She regrets being so rash and for taking out her frustration on her cousin. He is a good-natured boy, though prone to silliness. She will find a way to smooth things out with him later.

CHAPTER FOUR

"Rise and shine, Princess. Ya got ten minutes to get washed up and meet me in the cook tent, which is over there," said a big woman with pumpkin-coloured hair as she pointed her flabby arm out the door.

It took a few groggy seconds before I figured out she was talking to me. I sat up and squinted at her. Along with her funny accent and colourful hair, she wore a Hawaiian shirt that looked like a circus tent.

"Oh, by the way, I'm Bertha. Pleased ta meet ya. Now get up." Before I could say a word she turned and marched out of the tent.

"Pleased to meet ya, too," I mumbled. I looked around and found my bag sitting on the floor where Robbie had left it the night before. I knew Bertha said ten minutes, but I was much too tired to function at that speed. It took me nearly that long just to get off the bed.

When I finally stumbled into the kitchen tent, Bertha was moving around like a whirlwind. Other than the sound of bacon crackling on the frying pan, the camp was quiet as a graveyard. Probably because everyone else was in bed — where I should be.

"You're late. Over there're some eggs ta get crackin'. Make sure ya don't get shells in the mix or I might have to clobber ya. Catch my drift?" Bertha chuckled menacingly.

I wasn't worried that she'd actually clobber me — everyone knew that hitting kids was against the law — but if she ever did, I had the feeling I'd need someone to scrape me off the ground with a shovel.

I yawned. "I'm really tired. It took about fourteen hours to get here. And then falling asleep last night was almost impossible." Thanks to thunder butt sleeping next to me. "Then add to that the time change." It occurred to me that Mom, Aunt Margaret, and Uncle Stuart were still all curled up in bed.

"So you're tired, eh? Well you'll be happy to know I don't need ya after seven o'clock and ya can crash then."

I looked at my watch, which said six-thirty. "Well, that's not so bad. I guess I can hack it until then."

Bertha chuckled. "I was talkin' about seven tonight, dearie. Now get on with the eggs. I've got a schedule to keep here."

Ha! If she thought I was going to slog away in the kitchen for the next twelve hours, she had something to learn. I'd talk to Eddy. She'd put things right.

"I don't get what the rush is about. Other than you and me, no one else is even up yet," I said, then yawned again.

"That's right, Princess. But in about one hour there'll be about thirty people comin' through those doors over there and they'll be expectin' hot coffee and a hearty breakfast. Then after we're all cleaned up from breakfast we have just enough time to catch our breath and start all over again fer lunch. Now, if ya don't mind, I'd appreciate —" she glared at me and raised her voice "— if you'd get yer skinny rear end into gear so we don't let them down."

Whoa! It was time for a little name-dropping. "You probably don't know this, but my good friend, Dr. Edwina McKay — I call her Eddy, she's one of the professors here — got me this job. You see, I'm not really a cook's help. I'm actually aspiring to be an archaeologist, and Eddy's been training me."

"Well, you don't say. That's nice, eh?" Bertha said in a sort of friendly tone.

Good, now maybe things would go better, I thought. But then she picked up a wooden spoon and wagged it in my face.

"Now look here, Princess, let's get something straight. I don't give a chicken's waddle that this Dr. McKay is yer friend. I'm the boss of this here kitchen and the sooner ya accept it, the better things will be fer us all." She slapped the spoon on the counter with a crack. "So, now that we've got that straight, let's get the job done."

I could see that without Eddy to back me up I was on thin ice. I'd talk to her later, then Bertha would see who was boss.

Cracking open three dozen eggs carefully, I managed to get only a few shells in the bowl. "Okay, now what?"

"Add some milk, of course. I sure hope you're not one of those idjut helpers that has to be told what to do at every turn. Ya got a head, girl, use it. 'Sides, who doesn't know how to make scrambled eggs?"

I growled under my breath. Fine, if that was how it was going to be, I'd figure it out for myself. I mixed up the eggs and dumped in the jug of milk sitting on the counter. I wasn't sure if it needed the whole thing, but I always said too much was better than too little. I stirred the yellow mixture around, trying to think what else was supposed to go into scrambled eggs. I assumed everyone liked salt and pepper as much as I did, so I poured in a generous helping. Then I remembered that one time Aunt Margaret had made me Mexican-style eggs and they were really good. I hunted around for salsa, but couldn't find any. Then I spotted a little bottle of chili powder. The jar was half empty, but I poured in what was left and stirred some more.

"Have ya got the eggs ready?" Bertha shouted.

"Ready."

"Good, then bring them here, then get out to the dining hall and set the tables. We need napkins, cutlery, salt, and pepper. Now go!"

It crossed my mind to tell her that I had cleverly added the salt and pepper already, but then I figured the less I said the better. Just then I heard the skillet sizzle as Bertha poured out the eggs.

"What the heck! How much milk did ya use, girl?" Bertha shrieked. She turned to grab a towel and saw the empty milk jug on the counter. "Don't tell me ya used the whole thing! Have ya never made scrambled eggs before?"

"Well, I've eaten lots of them."

"Oh, fer Pete's sake, go to the cooler and grab me some more eggs that I can add to this mess. And don't be lookin' at me like that. Well? Go, girl, go."

After I helped mop up the runny eggs that had drained off the side of the grill and onto the floor, I burnt the toast, overfilled the coffee machine, and forgot to thaw the frozen butter. Just when I thought I'd messed up everything that I thought was possible, I dropped the plate of warm muffins on the floor as people started pouring into the dining hall. Probably a good thing they were there, because instead of yelling at me, the only thing that happened was Bertha's face went as red as the apples we set out in place of the muffins I dropped. I watched as she puffed and heaved like a steam engine.

"What ya gawkin' at, girl? Start servin' up the food."

As I plopped one spoonful of eggs after another onto plates, I searched the line, hoping to see Eddy. She needed to know there was a good reason why the last cook's help quit after one day. I needed her to get me out of here. There was no way I would survive two weeks of this, let alone three days.

"Hi, Peggy." I looked up and saw Robbie grinning at me. "Did you have a good sleep?"

I wasn't sure why, but the way she asked annoyed me. "Actually, it couldn't have been better. Thanks." Was that a moment of disappointment I'd seen on her face? Good.

"Maile, this is Peggy, the new help," Robbie said. Maile nodded at me. "She's the kid I was telling you about, the one who's friends with Dr. McKay." Obviously, my connection had impressed her. "You know, the one who knows everything about archaeology."

Zing! I might be a little slow at times, but I could totally tell that wasn't a compliment.

"Well, I didn't say I knew everything. I said I knew a considerable amount about archaeology. Certainly more than the average person," I shot back. Probably more than her and her friend, too, but I kept that to myself.

"And just how did you come by this considerable experience? You're how old?" Maile asked.

"Sorry, ladies, if ya don't mind, we need to keep the line movin'," Bertha told the girls. Then she turned to me. "And if ya don't mind, Princess, will ya hold off on all the chit-chat until social hour?"

"What do you mean? They're the ones —" I started to explain.

"Close yer gab hole, girl, and just keep the line movin'. These people have important work to do." Bertha smiled almost sweetly at Robbie and her friend. "Hot coffee's over there, ladies. Sorry 'bout the burnt toast. The help is new."

Robbie and her friend grinned. Now instead of Bertha, I was the one with the red face. I could tell there was no way to win this one, so I put my head down and didn't look up again until everyone had been served — everyone except Eddy. Where was she?

A little while later Bertha told me to set up a tub of warm rinsing water and then start collecting dirty dishes. As I made the rounds, I found that on nearly every plate, pushed to the side, were the scrambled eggs. I was thinking maybe this just wasn't a scrambled egg crowd. But later, when it was my turn to sit down to eat breakfast, I learned different. Wow! After one bite, my lips went numb. I must have put in a bit too much chili and pepper. I hoped no one knew I was responsible for the eggs that morning. When Bertha left the kitchen for a few minutes, I quickly scraped my eggs into the garbage along with the rest of the slop.

"Now that the breakfast rush is over I thought I'd take a little break and have a look around," I said when Bertha came back. "You know, see the site, check out the excavation —"

"Oh, a wee look around, eh?" She snorted. "Well, tink again, will ya? I've been run off me feet these past two days with no help a'tall … so I'm afraid yer little sightseein' trip will have to wait. Okay, Princess?"

"Is it just me, or do you call all your helpers 'Princess'? FYI — my name is Peggy," I said, gritting my teeth.

"Oh, sure it is — Princess Peggy," Bertha said slowly. "And FYI to ya, too. I've just tracked down that Dr. McKay of yours and gave her a piece of my mind. Did she even check to see if ya knew how to cook before gettin' ya this job? I tink not!" *Poor Eddy,* I thought. "And I don't know whatcha did to those eggs, but from now on ya don't go concoctin' something without my permission — got it?"

I sat down on the kitchen stool. "Well, I'm sorry I'm not what you expected. You should probably just look for a different helper." *Please look for a different helper,* I silently pleaded.

"Nope, too late fer that. 'Fraid I'm stuck with ya," Bertha said. "Ya might see yerself as the next star archaeologist, but fer now you're my helper. So get used to it. People say I'm the best cook around, and they also say I run my kitchen like it was the army — and that's true." She sat on the stool beside me and grinned. "But I'm a reasonable person, Princess."

She might be the best cook around here, but reasonable? I doubted that was true.

"Now I'm not makin' any promises," Bertha continued, "but if ya try yer best, then I'm willin' to put all this behind and start fresh." She stuck out her hand. "So is it a deal, Princess?"

At the moment what choice did I have? I took her hand and we shook on it.

"Good girl. Follow my lead and I might make a cook out of ya yet."

I could hear Aunt Margaret laughing now. "Oh, great," I said, hoping afterward that she hadn't noticed the hint of sarcasm. *No matter*, I thought, *the first chance I get I'm out of here.*

After scrubbing six trays, four pots, five muffin tins, and the entire grill by hand, I started peeling potatoes. The main course on the lunch menu was hearty potato-leek soup. There was also fresh dinner rolls, and bake-apple pie for dessert. I'd never seen bakeapples before. They were sort of like raspberries, but orangey and bigger. Bertha said they were an indigenous plant and grew all around L'Anse aux Meadows.

"Did the Vikings eat bakeapples?" I asked.

"I should tink they did," Bertha said. "After all, they weren't idjuts. They would've used whatever food was available. And I'm sure bakeapples were around back then just as they are today."

By the time the lunch crowd arrived, I'd had only a couple of minor disasters to test Bertha's temper. I was serving up soup — which actually tasted really good — when I heard a familiar voice coming from the crowd.

"Well, there you are," said Eddy, standing in line with a tray in hand.

"Eddy!" When she finally reached me, I asked, "Where have you been? I was looking for you this morning."

"I had a lot to get ready for my class, so I skipped breakfast." She bent over and whispered, "I guess we're

Gina McMurchy-Barber

both in hot water. I should have asked if you were any good at cooking before enlisting your help."

"You're right about that, Professor," Bertha chimed in when she caught us talking. "I can tell this one is a spitfire, but I tink we've come to an understandin'. After I rein her in some, she might make a good cook's helper, after all." Bertha winked at Eddy, who looked sheepish. "Okay, Princess Peggy, ya done well. Now go have lunch with yer friend."

"Really? Thanks." She didn't have to tell me twice. I ripped off my apron, grabbed a tray, and helped myself to lunch. When I got to the table where Eddy sat, there were no free chairs. She pointed to the table behind her. "Hey, people, this here is my young friend, Peggy Henderson. She's working as cook's help for the duration of field school. But she's keen about archaeology and will no doubt be making her way around our site from time to time. Feel free to share what you've learned."

"From what I hear, she already knows everything," Robbie said, smirking. I wanted to sneer, too, but with all the other students looking at me I decided it was better if I pretended I hadn't heard her remark. After introductions no one took any notice of me.

"Professor McKay, I was wondering what sampling method you preferred?" asked a short and very hairy guy.

"Well, Taylor, every archaeology site is unique, and the kind of sampling you do will actually all come down to how much time and money you have."

"Sometimes sampling isn't even possible," I chimed in. "Like when you have an emergency excavation that

58

needs to be done right away. Right, Eddy?" Taylor looked annoyed. "Did you already cover that topic yet, Eddy?"

"No, we haven't got to salvage archaeology yet, Peggy," Eddy answered.

"Oh … well, in that case," I said, turning to Taylor, "real-life archaeology is messy, Taylor. Take the time I worked on an ancient Coast Salish excavation site where the property owner was building a pond in the backyard. In that case there was no way the lady living there was going to let us dig up samples all over her yard." I didn't see the point in telling him that it happened to be my Aunt Margaret's yard. Why wreck a good story? "Then there was the time Eddy and I were called out to excavate an abandoned historical cemetery some teen vandalized — again, no chance to do sampling because you —"

"Professor McKay, by my watch it's time we got back to work," Professor Brant butted in. "These students can continue this discussion in the field. We don't want them to think the cook's helper is here to educate them on the finer details of archaeology, do we?"

Whoa, he just cut me off in the middle of my sentence. Jerk!

Eddy glanced at me, and I could tell she thought I might blurt out something. "Thank you, everyone. This has been a good discussion. And I might add a delicious lunch. But you're correct, Professor, we should get back to work." Eddy pushed her chair back. "You'll all be happy to know we're heading out to a small site this afternoon. We'll practise setting our datum point and then do some surveying." Eddy waved at me. "See you later, Peggy."

Datum points, surveying, excavating … sounded like fun. As they left, I looked around the dining hall at all the dirty dishes and sighed.

"Please, Aunt Gudrid, ask Uncle to take me on the Viking," begs Sigrid. "I could help as a lookout or do the cooking."

Aunt Gudrid laughs. "Cooking! I can hardly get you to help me now with the cooking. How will things be different on the Viking?" She shakes her head. "No, Sigrid. With half the men gone, everyone in the settlement is needed to watch for the skraelings. In particular, I need you to watch over Snorri."

"Snorri! It's always about him!" shouts Sigrid. "He's not my child. He's yours. Why do I always get stuck with him?" It is obvious that Gudrid is ignoring her. "Fine, I'll ask Uncle Thorfinn myself to take me."

"I've explained a hundred times that Thorfinn won't take you. He's only taking a handful of his best men and one of the smaller trade knarrs, so there's no place for a demanding and belligerent girl." Gudrid waves her off. "I'm done with this conversation. I must help prepare the ship. As for you, you'll do what you're told, young lady. And, yes, that means taking care of your cousin. And by the way, it smells like he's soiled his trousers."

Sigrid grits her teeth and kicks up a small dust cloud from the floor. When Uncle Thorfinn and Aunt Gudrid told her two and a half years ago they were going to the settlement Lucky Leif discovered in the new world, she was excited. She was sure it was going to be an adventure — seeing new worlds, discovering treasures to bring back to Greenland, and maybe even a chance to fight in battles.

She had never been on a Viking, and certainly had never been on the open ocean where there are no landmarks to follow for days and days. It was here where she learned how seafaring Norsemen relied on things like the sun and the stars, the colour of the water, the direction of the waves, and even birds to point them toward land.

When they first set out on the Viking, no one knew that Aunt Gudrid would soon have a baby. During the voyage, a few of the other women and youths suffered from seasickness, but no one spent more time hanging over the side of the ship than Gudrid. The baby was born soon after they arrived at the small abandoned settlement Leif had built years before when he named the place Vinland.

At first baby Snorri was special, partly because he was the first Norse child to be born in this new world. Sigrid was happy for her aunt and uncle who had waited for a long time to have a child. And, of course, she was delighted to have a new cousin. He was fun to have around — like a kitten or a pup. But the novelty soon wore off as she was left being responsible for his care more and more.

Then the disagreement with the skraelings began. These people, who lived on the land long before the Norsemen had arrived, were vicious and unpredictable savages. Because of them Sigrid was saddled with the care of the youngster and always left out of exciting things like the Viking trips. On top of that, Uncle Thorfinn was either too busy or too tired to keep his promise to teach her to use the sword.

"It's for my own safety," she pleaded a while ago.

"You're hardly big enough to hold the thing let alone fight with it," he said, laughing. "If it's really your safety you're worried about, you're better off learning to use a dagger, girl."

With all the trouble with the skraelings, Uncle Thorfinn questions whether staying in the new world is worth the danger and effort, especially with a toddler to protect. If this next Viking does not prove profitable, the settlers and crew may load up the ships to the brim with timber, furs, and whatever fruits or vegetables they have gained and set sail for Greenland when the warm winds return.

Until then the clan that are left at the settlement will hunt, gather, and store the food they will need for their third winter. When food has been dried and stored, there is still the work of repairing the ships. Many rivets need replacing, fresh pitch to apply, and torn sails to sew.

After Thorfinn's knarr sets sail and disappears around the point, Sigrid corners her cousin, Gunnar. "If you practise the sword with me, I'll sneak you some cloudberry juice," she promises.

"And what about him?" Gunnar asks, pointing at Snorri. "What if he tells?"

"Him? He can hardly say anything. He's nothing to be concerned about. Do we have an agreement?"

Gunnar nods.

"Good. I'll meet you on the battlefield when Aunt Gudrid is busy at the forge."

"The battlefield? And where might that be?"

"The clearing just past the big trees, of course."

"And what about skraelings? Aren't you afraid they might come?"

"Me, afraid? I pity the skraeling who dares to challenge me. I relish the idea of skewering one of those scoundrels. On the other hand, perhaps you're the one who's afraid."

"Of course not." Gunnar turns a dark shade of red.

"Good. Then I'll see you on the shore after chores are done." Sigrid grabs Snorri by the hand and leads him out back to change his stinky trousers.

"Where have you been you lazy girl? I've been stirring this cloudberry wine so long that my arm feels like it will fall off," says Aunt Gudrid as Sigrid takes her place at the fire. While her aunt makes busy with other tasks, Sigrid secretly pours small amounts of the fragrant juice into a skin flask for Gunnar.

That afternoon Sigrid asks her aunt, "Am I allowed to relieve myself?"

"Sigrid, while I expect you to be helpful to me, you're not a thrall," says Aunt Gudrid. "Only slaves need to ask permission to go anywhere."

Just as Sigrid is almost out the door, her aunt calls after her, "Take Snorri with you. And be quick. There's still much to do."

Sigrid snatches the youngster by the hand and dashes out of the house and into the fresh air.

"Come, you little pest. We have to hurry." Sigrid begins to run, conscious that Snorri's feet are barely touching the ground as she drags him along. They run past the wood shop and out toward the seashore, far from her aunt's peering eyes and beyond calling range. She giggles, knowing that in a short while her aunt will wonder where she is and will not be able to find her anywhere nearby. Aunt Gudrid will then become angry, but any consequence is worth the chance to practise sword fighting.

When Gunnar sees her, he yells, "Did you bring it?"

"No, silly. It isn't even ready yet. You'll get it. I promise," Sigrid tells him. "Did you bring me a sword?"

The boy holds up a gleaming blade. "Will this do? It was my grandfather's. He named it Skull-Splitter." Gunnar's chest heaves with pride, as if he were the only Norseman to own a weapon with such a name.

Sigrid's hand trembles as she takes the sword. Then she draws out the iron blade from the fleece-lined scabbard covered in deerskin and admires the intricate silver-and-copper inlay along the blade. She throws off her cape and apron and pushes up her sleeves.

"Snorri, you sit here and watch. And if you don't get in the way, I may give you a treat." Turning to Gunnar, she says, "All right, let us begin ..."

CHAPTER FIVE

"Okay, Princess, you're free to wander about and have yerself a wee look-see," offered Bertha. "But be back here by four-thirty or I'll clobber ya. Catch my drift?"

I guess she'd taken pity on me. Right after lunch we'd started preparations for dinner — the menu was broccoli-and-macaroni casserole, garden salad, biscuits, and apple crumble for dessert.

"I'm goin' to grate cheese and you'll fry up the onions," said Bertha.

Sounded simple enough. I turned on the stove, got out the big pan, and poured in some oil. Then I started chopping up an onion.

"Eh, what the heck are ya doin'?" shrieked Bertha. "Don't ya know ya never leave hot oil on the stove unattended? This is the kind of thing that can cause a kitchen fire. Let's get this straight, Princess. Never leave something cookin' on the stove without keepin' a close eye on it and never let oil get too hot. Got it?"

Geez, she didn't have to make such a big deal. I only had my back turned for a few minutes.

Finally, the casserole was ready for the oven, the salad good to go. Bertha wanted to make the crumble herself — she said it was her specialty.

"But you're in charge of the biscuits. They're not hard

to make, so I'm sure ya can handle it, right?" Bertha said, though I wasn't sure she really did believe I could handle it. But biscuits didn't sound hard. After all, they were basically just flour and water.

By the time I got out of the cook tent, it was raining. I pulled on my raincoat and headed out across the meadow to find Eddy and the others. I wanted to see just what these students were learning. With all of my experience I was sure I could teach them a trick or two.

The nippy easterly wind whipped my hair out from under my hood. It was cold enough that I half thought about going back for the mittens Aunt Margaret had given me. Instead, I tucked my hands inside my coat and gazed at the white-capped waves. With a little imagination I could almost see Viking ships in the bay, along with the burly bearded men who had sailed them a thousand years ago.

"Eddy!" I shouted when I saw her far off. She didn't hear me, so I ran over to her. When I got there, she was with a few students and kneeling inside a two-metre pit, pointing to the sides.

"You can see how these layers of stratigraphy are like layers of time. Each new colour in the soil represents a different geological and historical period," Eddy explained. I snickered at the students who were madly writing down every word she said in their notebooks. "These layers can help us to determine how old the human remains or artifact might be. That's why it's so important to never remove —"

"An artifact from the site until you've measured, recorded, and photographed it," I jumped in. "Did you tell them what in situ means, Eddy? It's Latin for 'in place.' Just remember, the farther down in the soil you go, the farther back in time you're going. Kind of like time travelling!" While I thought my analogy was clever, I heard someone groan.

"That's correct, Peggy." Eddy smiled for a moment and then turned back to the students. "Now I'd like you all to use your notebooks to make a sketch of the stratigraphy layers, and while you're at it, keep in mind the colour and texture of each layer and what period in time they represent."

"You didn't mean me, right, Eddy?" I said. "I don't have a notebook, but of course I know all this stuff about stratigraphy, anyway. Is there anyone who wants my help?" That time I definitely heard someone groan.

"Peggy, did you know there's a Kids Explorers program here at L'Anse aux Meadows?" Robbie asked. "Since you've nothing better to do, you could go over to the main centre and sign up." Someone in the group giggled. "If you're good, you'll even get a booklet filled with fun activities. You can earn a certificate and reward, too. You should check it out, like maybe right now."

"Ah, Peggy, maybe you would enjoy seeing some of the other parts of the site," Eddy suggested. "We can chat later when I'm finished teaching, okay?" I could feel everyone's eyes on me and hated that they could see what must have looked like a face splattered in tomato sauce.

I slunk away and headed toward the replica Norse settlement. I didn't know why Eddy didn't want me to stay and help her, or why Robbie was always so obnoxious. Kids Explorers program — I had just turned thirteen, not six!

I followed the boardwalk toward the Viking settlement. All around were low-growing plants and shrubs. I thought one of them was the bakeapple — at least it had the small orange berries Bertha had shown me in the kitchen. I plucked a berry off and popped it into my mouth, then shivered. Boy, was it tart!

At the settlement there was a small group of tourists crowded around a Viking guy. I knew he was just acting the part, but with his shaggy blond hair, sheepskin vest, and woollen pants he looked really authentic.

"Most people tink the Vikings were a dirty bunch. But I tink they must've been clean freaks," he said. "Why else were so many tweezers, razors, and combs found around the site?" The guy sounded a bit Irish. Kind of like Bertha, only she spoke much louder. Must be the Newfoundland accent Mom had told me about.

The guide held up a piece of stringy tree bark. "Here's one dirty little fact most folks don't know. The Norsemen would take some of this touchwood fungus here, let it marinate in human urine fer several days —"

"They soaked it in pee? Gross!" yelled a kid in the tour group.

The guide laughed. "Now wait a minute. Let me finish. After that they boiled the urine and fungus fer many days, then took it out and pounded it into flat mats. Now comes the really good part. When they went on a voyage, they could light this stuff on fire. And instead of burnin', it would smoulder fer days and days. This clever invention meant they'd have fire any time they needed it right there on the ships." There were murmurs of approval from the group.

"Those Vikings were real *wizz*-ards," I said. A few people in the group chuckled at my pun.

"Good one," said the guide, smiling. "Feel free to join our tour, young lady — *urine* good company." More snickering.

"Thanks. Pee jokes aside, are you an expert on the Vikings?" I asked.

"I suppose it depends on who you're talkin' to. I was born and raised a stone's throw from here. When I was a boy, they discovered this place. I often came and watched the archaeologists — that's Helge Ingstad and his wife, Anne Stine Ingstad — excavatin' this site back in the 1960s."

"That's cool. I'm going to be an archaeologist. In fact, that's why I'm here."

"Oh, I see. You're one of the students then?" asked the guide.

"Well, no, not exactly. I'm too young to join the university class. But I know enough about archaeology to talk for hours."

The man looked confused. "So if you're not a student, then you're a tourist?"

"Actually, I'm the cook's help. I help make the meals for the archaeology field school."

"Oh, I see. So you're helpin' Bertha. She's a fine cook, though a bit of a hothead at times, and I'm not just talkin' about her red hair, either."

I nodded, glad that someone else knew what I had to put up with.

"So ya like to cook, eh?"

"Actually, I'm a terrible cook and just as bad at being a cook's helper. I took the job so I could come here and learn about the Vikings and be part of an excavation of the site. My friend, Eddy, she's one of the field school professors. She got me the job."

"Ah, I tink I met that friend of yers — white-haired ol' lady with a vest full of pockets. Some might mistake her fer somebody's little ol' grandma instead of an archaeologist."

Eddy was sort of old and was a grandma, but I never thought of her as a "little ol' grandma." "Don't be fooled by her appearance. She's strong and smart. And I bet she knows more about archaeology than anyone here."

"Well, of course — must be why they asked her to come here and teach. So what's yer name, young lady?"

"I'm Peggy Henderson."

"Good to meet ya, Peggy. I'm John Austin." He turned to the others. "Well, c'mon then, let's all go into the great house. Mind yer heads as we go through the entrance."

The outside of the building looked more like a little grassy hill than someone's house. As we passed through the thick portal, I ran my hand over the rough sod bricks piled neatly one on the other. Even the floor was made of hard, beaten-down earth. It was toasty warm inside, and the place smelled like greasy fish and smoke. After my eyes adjusted to the dimness, I saw the main room was narrow and long, with a roaring fire in the centre hearth. Hanging above it was a cooking pot with steam rising to the ceiling. I figured that was where the weird smell was coming from.

"Hello, Svanhilda and Runa," said John to a woman and a girl who seemed about my age. They were both dressed in old-fashioned Norse costumes. "We have some guests here who'd like to see the inside of yer home. Can we come in?"

"Hello, John," the lady said. "By all means, bring yer guests in and we'll give 'em a look around. Might there be anyone who'd like to try on a Viking helmet or hold a sword and shield today?"

My arm shot up. The only other person who showed interest in trying them out was a little kid.

"Yay! Me first," he said, jumping up and down excitedly. "Little kids first, right?" His parents looked as if they were about to scold him.

The lady smiled down at him. "Did you know we have a rule here that ladies go first?" The kid frowned. Then she turned to me. "Would you like to go first, dear?"

I realized everyone was staring at me, and my face suddenly felt like melting wax again. "No, that's all right. He can go."

The kid put the helmet on, and his parents laughed when it swallowed his entire head. Then he struggled to lift the sword with his two hands. "That's heavy," he announced. "I bet my daddy could lift it." The boy glanced up at his father standing nearby.

"Okay, Fynn, you've had your turn. Let someone else try."

Yah, Fynn — scram and let me have a turn. I didn't want to let on, but I was excited, too. Still, I waited until the tourists wandered off to different corners of the house. Then I pulled the deep, bowl-shaped helmet over my head. It felt as heavy as a brick, and hard, too. I picked up the giant Frisbee-shaped shield. It had a wide leather handle, but that didn't make holding on to it any easier. Finally, I was ready for the sword. I wrapped my hand around the grip. It took a lot of strength to lift the blade and point it. After only a few seconds, the weight of the sword forced my arm to shake, and I had to let it drop.

"I can't imagine how they ran into battle holding all this stuff." I said to Svanhilda.

"You're right, it is heavy," she said. "Back then the men wouldn't have been so tall as nowadays and most certainly not as handsome, but one thing's fer sure, they were a strong bunch."

"What about the women? Did they wear all this stuff, too?" I asked.

"Women?" She laughed. "Warrin', raidin', and tradin' were men's work, my dear. Havin' said that, there were a few women who traded in the apron fer a sword. They called them shield maidens. But make no mistake, choosin' such a life would've been hard. It meant turnin' their backs on their families fer a life most likely to end tragically."

"I'm guessing any woman who became a warrior must have been some kind of a hulk, like Xena, the Warrior Princess."

"I can't say any were like Xena, but I do recall there were a few fierce lassies. Can't recall their names just now."

I had a dozen more questions, but then John called for our attention.

"Okay, folks, you'll probably want to see the gallery in the main centre. If ya head up there now before we close fer the day, you'll have enough time to watch the video about the Vikings who once lived here. Tanks fer comin', and I hope ya enjoyed the tour." As John ushered the tourists out the small doorway, he signalled that I should wait.

"Before ya go, I wanted to introduce ya to Renee and her daughter, Louise. Ladies, this is Peggy. She's going to be around fer the next while helpin' Bertha cook fer the archaeology field school."

Renee — otherwise known as Svanhilda up to a few minutes ago — looked at John with knowing eyes. "Well, good on ya. Bet Bertha will keep ya on yer toes." She and John had a little chuckle.

"Peggy's not just an ordinary cook's help," John added. "She's really here because she's interested in archaeology and wants to learn more about the Vikings."

"Ya are?" said the girl. "I'm interested in archaeology, too. That's the only reason I agreed to help my ma here at the Meadows. I'm goin' to be an expert on Vikings."

"Louise, it would be nice if ya showed Peggy around sometime," suggested her mother.

"Would ya like that? I know my way around here like it was my own backyard."

I couldn't have been happier. I was standing in front of a Newfoundland version of myself. "That would be awesome. It would sure beat being alone."

"Alone? Ya mean ya don't like to hang out with the archaeology students? I sure would. I'd pick their brains," Louise said.

"Well, first of all they don't want me around. And secondly, I don't think there's much in their brains to pick."

Renee laughed. "Let's hope that's not true. I've noticed they don't seem much interested in us, either. I suppose they're just too busy. Pity, because the guides here know plenty. Like Niko Ekstrom, over at the forge.

He's a Viking saga expert. He could tell ya 'bout them shield maidens, too, if ya want to know more."

"Really? I'd like to talk to him." Talking to the friendly guides was a nice change from the cold shoulders I was getting from the field school students. "Would I be able to talk to him now?"

John looked at his watch. "I see it's nearly five o'clock. I'm afraid he's gone home by now."

"It's five already? Agh! I'm late. Bertha's going to kill me." I grabbed my raincoat and headed for the door.

"Don't worry 'bout Bertha," called out Renee. "Her bark's worse than her bite — usually."

As I headed into the wind, I was sure I heard laughter coming from inside the sod house.

"I'm tired and I've had enough," whines Gunnar.

"Don't be so feeble. We just got started," Sigrid says.

"Just started? Take a look at the setting sun." He points to the horizon where the sun is nothing but a sliver, nearly fallen down behind the hill. "My mother will be wondering where I am. We don't want her coming to look for us. If she knows what we've been up to, we'll be flogged for certain."

Sigrid sighs. "All right. But tomorrow we must practise again. I can feel that I'm making progress. We should hide the sword somewhere nearby."

"Sigrid, where's Snorri? Gunnar's eyes are wide as he searches the meadow and the nearby beach.

"Snorri?" Sigrid realizes she has not even thought about him since the moment she picked up the sword. Where could he be? He could not have gone that far — after all, he is only a toddler. "Snorri!" she calls again and again. As the minutes

pass with no sight of the little boy, Sigrid's pulse quickens. "Snorri! You little menace, if you're hiding, you come out right now or I'll —" What will she do? It is not his fault that she completely ignored him or forgot to keep an eye on him. She gazes out to the grey, cold ocean with its choppy waves, then to the marshlands to the west and the forest beyond that.

"Quickly, Gunnar," Sigrid commands. "You go to the beach. I'll head into the forest." The two go in opposite directions, calling out the little boy's name.

As the minutes mount, Sigrid grows more frightened. What will Aunt Gudrid do to me? she thinks. "Snorri, where are you?" It seems unlikely he could cross the wetlands without getting stuck. Perhaps he has fallen down and is trapped in the mud. "Why can't I hear you crying? Cry, Snorri, cry for help," she wills him.

Sigrid reaches the crest of the hill and looks back to where she has come from. Gunnar is there, waving and beckoning her to return. Maybe he has found him, she thinks. She races over the dense, wet ground, tripping every few feet. Each time she falls, her dress gets wetter and heavier and causes her to stumble even more.

"There's no sign of him. I think we need to get help," says Gunnar.

It will be dark soon, and Sigrid knows what he says is true. As they run to the settlement, Sigrid's mind flashes images of tiny Snorri in the hands of a wild cat or drowned in the sea or marsh, or even worse, fallen into the hands of the wicked skraelings.

Silently, she prays to Frigga — I know I cursed you before, and I am very sorry for that. But, Great Goddess, do not take out your anger on Snorri. Please watch over him.

Show us where to find him. If you do this, then I promise to become the woman you want me to be. And if you absolutely insist, I will marry that old man Uncle Thorfinn has chosen and have a child of my own one day … probably … most likely. But only if no harm comes to Snorri!

Through the dark night, every man and woman from the settlement searches meadow, hillside, and beach for Snorri. His name is called so often it becomes one with the wind. The search continues until the day breaks. But the only son of Gudrid and Thorfinn is nowhere to be found. Sigrid cannot look any of the settlers in the eye for the shame of her neglect. "Poor Snorri," she cries.

"It was the skraelings, I'm sure," wails Gudrid. "They took him from me. What have they done with my little boy?"

"Wait, what's that there?" one of the men calls out. He points to a thin line of smoke rising from the forest. They all turn and see it.

"Skraelings!" screams Hanna, Gunnar's mother. "Skraelings have started a fire in the forest. What are they doing?"

The men who are already with shield and sword charge up the hillside first. Gudrid and Sigrid follow close behind. Once inside the woods they smell the fire and follow the scent. As they come to a small clearing, though, they do not find an unchecked blaze but only a small firepit with flames licking up the last of the night.

"Wait here!" commands Hellava, one of the men. "I don't know what we'll find."

Gudrid whimpers, and Sigrid holds her hand as Hellava approaches the fire.

With a burst of energy Hellava calls to her, "Come, Gudrid, come quick."

Sigrid and her aunt run toward him. When they arrive, they look down on a sight more peculiar than can be imagined. Next to the fire, lying on a bed of moss and covered in a deerskin, is Snorri, peacefully asleep. Only when Gudrid speaks his name does he open his eyes. He smiles and yawns, not a care on his mind.

"But who? Who did this?" sobs Gudrid as she buries her face in Snorri's neck.

"It was Frigga who saved him," Sigrid announces. "I prayed to her and she has saved Snorri. She saved him from the beasts and the savages. Thank you, Frigga." Sigrid falls to the forest floor in a heap of relief.

A moment later Snorri lifts his sleepy head. That is when they notice for the first time the streak of red paint that reaches from his forehead to his chin. He smiles again and opens his chubby little hand, revealing a small, carved charm.

Gudrid gasps. "What does this mean?" she whispers.

In the following weeks no one speaks of the ordeal, and Sigrid is a perfect helpmate to her aunt. Not once does she argue or shirk her duties. Never does she begrudge caring for Snorri, nor take her eyes off him when they are outside the home. And not for a moment does Sigrid forget the dreadful promise she made to Frigga, but she is no longer certain that it was the goddess who saved the boy.

I burst into the kitchen, half expecting Bertha to be standing there ready to chuck tomatoes at me. Miraculously, she wasn't around. I hit the floor running.

"Biscuits, biscuits. What's in biscuits?" I asked out loud. Flour! I ran to the pantry and hauled out the bag of flour. "How much?" After a nanosecond, I decided ten cups would do. "Okay, what next? Water."

Taking the large metal mixing bowl over to the sink, I turned on the tap and let the water run until it looked about right — not that I knew what looked right. "Okay, what now? Stir it, you idjut," I said, hearing Bertha in my mind. I grabbed the nearest spoon and started mixing the flour and water. A recipe might have been helpful, but I kind of remembered Great-Aunt Beatrix teaching me once to make baking powder biscuits. "Ah, right … baking powder," I said. "But how much?" I took the new box of baking powder off the shelf. It was only a small box — hopefully it was enough.

After dumping it all in, I continued mixing. Then I got the idea to shred some cheese to add flavour. Aunt Margaret did that sometimes. I knew it would be only minutes before Bertha burst through the door. "Oven! Turn on the oven, Peggy." I flipped the dial to three hundred and fifty degrees. Then thought better and turned it to four hundred and fifty. Then I suddenly remembered the chili I'd burned at home and turned it back to three hundred and fifty.

While the oven got hot I buttered a few baking sheets and then plopped scoops of the biscuit mixture onto them. They weren't uniform in size, but what the heck — it would give people a choice of small, medium, or large.

Miraculously, I slid the sheets into the oven just as Bertha came through the door. That was close.

"Well, good. There's me tinking I'd arrive and ya wouldn't be here." She peeked through the oven door.

"They're not very attractive, girl, but never mind. Looks aren't everything." She put on her apron and washed her hands. "Okay, don't be standin' with yer gob open like an idjut. Go and set the tables. Go on. I'll watch over yer biscuits and won't let them burn."

Ten minutes later people began filling the dining hall. When the timer sounded, I went to the oven and took out my biscuits. Whoa — every one of them was the size of an extra-big muffin. Maybe that just meant they were extra-fluffy. I set the first batch next to Bertha's stew. Her eyes widened at the sight of them. When I took out the second sheet, I decided to try one. I chomped down, but it was so tough and chewy my teeth couldn't even tear through it. Then came a funny, bitter taste. Yuck!

"C'mon, Princess, bring them here. We're running out of the first batch." I chucked the one I'd tasted into the garbage. If possible, I would have done the same with the rest of them, but Bertha kept waving at me to bring them over.

As the students and professors lined up for their suppers, I felt a little jealous listening to them chatting excitedly about their day.

"Did you manage to get signed up for the kiddy program, Peggy?" I looked up to see Robbie and Maile smirking at me. "Don't look so serious, kid. I'm just joking."

When Robbie helped herself to a large biscuit, I nearly bit my lip. Boy, I'd sure like to see the expression on her face when she stuffed it in her gob. Then I saw Eddy in the line.

"Peggy, I'm sorry about this afternoon," Eddy said quietly when she reached the counter. "When I'm teaching, I really need to give my full attention to the students. You understand, right?"

"Sure," I said, even though I didn't really get what the big deal was if I dropped in on her while she was teaching.

"This evening we're having a talk from one of the local experts. I thought you might like to join."

"A talk about what?"

"Viking sagas and folklore," Eddy said. "I've enlisted the help of one of the guides from the site. It will be very interesting. Will you come?"

"Is the expert named Niko Ekstrom?"

She smiled at me, the way she always did when I surprised her. "You know about him?"

I nodded. "Heard about him, that's all." I glanced over at the table where Robbie was wrestling with her biscuit, and I nearly laughed out loud. "I'd really like to come, but will that upset anyone?"

"No, I'm sure it will be fine. So I'll see you in the main centre around seven, okay?"

I was so happy I nearly floated around the kitchen.

After dinner I went out to the tables to gather up the dirty dishes. And on every plate, pushed to the side, were biscuits, small, medium, and large.

"This is turning into a habit, girl," said Bertha when she came out from the kitchen to help me clear up. "Show me yer recipe."

"Ah, well, I didn't use a recipe. I like to just wing it when I'm cooking."

Bertha's eyes opened to the size of baseballs. "Wing it? There's no wingin' it in my kitchen ... unless you're a chicken headin' fer the oven." She picked up one of the leftover biscuits and took a bite, or at least tried. "Ack … these things are like rubber. If this is what ya get fer wingin' it, from now on —"

Just when Bertha was in the middle of blasting me there was a knock at the kitchen door. It was Professor Brant, the director of the field school. He asked Bertha to step outside with him. I couldn't hear what they were saying, but there was no mistaking that Bertha was upset. When she came back into the room, her pinched red face confirmed it.

"Well, His Highness isn't too pleased about the food, and I can't say I blame him. He as much as said we either get our act together or he's goin' to find someone else fer the job."

Instantly, I felt like celebrating and would have started doing the victory dance if it hadn't been for the look on Bertha's face. She sat down on the stool with a thump.

"The biscuits were my fault — and the eggs," I said. "There's no reason for you to lose your job."

"I won't deny that, but it seems he didn't much like the broccoli in with the macaroni, either." She pulled a cloth out of her apron pocket and dabbed at her eyes. "My husband's out of work, and I've got two daughters to put through college. I've been countin' on this money to help us get by."

If I got fired, I'd spend my time learning about Vikings, wandering around L'Anse aux Meadows, and hanging out with Eddy. Maybe I could even move in with her and finally get a decent sleep. It would be like the perfect vacation. But when I watched Bertha wiping tears off her face, my heart went soft. I didn't want to see her lose her job, especially since she really needed it.

Bertha reached into a drawer, pulled out a box, and handed it to me. "From now on ya don't cook or bake a thing unless ya get the recipe from here — understand? And not only that, ya must follow it to the tee. Get me, Princess?"

I nodded. "I promise. From now on no more winging it."

"That's a good girl. Run along then. I'll finish up here." I looked around at all the dirty pots and pans that were left from dinner and opened my mouth to object. "No, I tink I need to have a bit of time alone. It'll be fine. Go see yer friend."

An hour ago if she'd told me to leave I'd be out of there so fast they'd have to give me a ticket for speeding. But now things were different. I might be the cause of Bertha losing her job. And by now the professor had probably blasted Eddy for recommending me as the cook's help. I bet everyone else, like Robbie, knew about it, too.

I looked out to the Atlantic Ocean. It reminded me of home — only home was about eight thousand kilometres away. Whenever I needed a place to think, I went to the beach. As the waves washed away footsteps in the sand, they washed away bad feelings, too. I glanced at the sign that read BIRCHY NUDDICK TRAIL AND BEACH THIS WAY. So just like that I was off to find myself a log by the shore. With any luck I'd have the place to myself.

CHAPTER SIX

Fog was rolling in from off the water, and the damp air nipped at my ears and seeped inside my sweater. Not far offshore floated an iceberg as big as a ship. I watched it silently pass by.

"Ya should've been here a month ago. There were almost as many icebergs as fishin' ships."

I leaped off the log and spun around to find the girl I'd met in the Viking sod house. Only now she was dressed like a normal kid.

"That one there's about half the size of the one that sank the *Titanic*."

"What?" I blurted.

"You've heard of the *Titanic*, right? Sank about six hundred kilometres off Newfoundland's shore in 1912. The berg that sank her was half the size of the one you're gawkin' at."

"Oh." I slumped down on the log again.

"Remember me?" she asked.

"Runa, right?" I said. I wasn't much in the mood for talking at that moment and hoped she'd act like an iceberg and float away.

"That's just my work name when I'm playin' the part of a Viking kid. My real name's Louise. So what'er ya doin'?" she pried.

"Just looking." Obviously, Louise wasn't going anywhere soon, so I finally asked, "What are you doing?"

"I'm scoutin'."

"Scouting? You mean like 'Scout's honour,' 'be prepared,' 'build your own fire and shelter,' that kind of stuff?"

Louise laughed. "Not that kind of scoutin'. I like to hunt around, see if I can find something old, something the archaeologists missed. Want to look with me?"

I snorted. "You seriously think this place hasn't already been picked over with a magnifying glass?"

"So I take it that means you're not interested. That's fine." Louise scooted past me and started up the trail. "Too bad, 'cause I found something, and it's pretty big."

As I watched her go, I suddenly panicked. What if — no matter how slim the chances might be — she really had found something? It might be my only opportunity to do something even remotely related to archaeology.

I jumped up. "Wait. I'll come with you," I said, trying to sound only a little interested. She didn't stop, just waved at me to hurry. We headed up the same boardwalk trail that led to the main centre.

"We're not going *there*, are we?" I asked, suddenly worried Eddy would see me. If she did, I knew she'd do everything possible to get me to join the group for the lecture.

"Why? Do ya want to go there? They've got Niko Ekstrom talkin' to the archaeology students tonight about Norse sagas. That's a first. They usually ignore us folks who play the part of the Vikings. I guess they don't tink we know too much. So, anyway, ya want to go hear him?"

"Ah, no. I don't want to go. You?"

"No, I can talk to old Niko any day I like. Besides, I've already heard lots of his stories." She smiled and looked off to the north. "Actually, if you're comin' with me, we're headin' up there." She pointed to the rocky hillside. "It's a bit of a hike, but I found some cool pictographs."

"Wait, the Vikings didn't make pictographs."

Louise looked offended. "The Vikings? Don't be an idjut. Of course, they didn't. They carved rune symbols into stone tablets. It was the First Nations people. They're the ones who left pictographs. Pictographs are —"

"I know what pictographs are," I blurted, now the one who felt insulted. "They're images painted onto stone surfaces, not to be confused with petroglyphs, which are carvings on stone surfaces."

"Good thing you're not a complete fool. That gets borin' real fast."

"Ouch. That hurt."

Louise laughed while the wind whipped up strands of her long red hair. She turned and began to climb up the trail that led to the hills. "I'm just foolin' with ya, Peggy. One thing I bet ya didn't know was a thousand years ago this hillside was covered in trees and the Beothuk lived here."

"Well, that makes sense," I said. "Where I live, it was the Coast Salish who occupied Crescent Beach first. They were there about five thousand years before Europeans arrived."

"Coast Salish. Huh? I tink I'd like to know more about them people. Fer now let's see what the Beothuks were up to. C'mon, follow me."

She climbed ahead as nimbly as a mountain goat while I struggled to keep up. As we went higher, the buildings of L'Anse aux Meadows began to shrink in the distance. Funny, I'd come all the way to Newfoundland so I could find out more about the Vikings. Instead here I was on my way to see a First Nations site.

Within minutes Louise was so far ahead I'd lost sight of her. But now and then I heard her calling my name, so I continued to follow her voice. When I arrived at the top of the hill, there was a large rock overhang. Out of breath, I sat down to admire more icebergs floating in the distance.

Then Louise called my name again. This time it sounded hollow. "In here, Peggy. I'm in the cave."

I turned toward the sound of her voice, which came from a small opening at the base of the rock. It was hidden so well I would never have noticed it on my own.

Just before I stuck my head into the narrow entry a startling thought crossed my mind. This would be a perfect place for a wolf or bear den. "Louise? I don't think this looks safe."

"Hah. I didn't take ya fer a coward!"

That stung. "I'm not a coward. It's called being cautious. Sorry that I'd rather not be some bear's dinner when it finds me here." I heard my voice enter into the cave and echo. Before it even finished reverberating, Louise's giggles echoed back at me.

"Don't be silly. It's safe. I checked already. If this was a bear's den, then why isn't there any dung or bones from animals eaten? I promise there's nothin' like that here, but I guarantee you'll want to see what is."

Only a bit reassured, I edged into the narrow entry not much wider than a street manhole. I followed the light coming from Louise's flashlight. "How did you ever find this?" When I came into the main cavern, a chill went up the back of my neck.

"Cool, eh?" said Louise.

Without looking at her I could tell she was smiling — and no wonder. The walls of the cave were covered in pictures. They were simple stick figures, and though they looked really old, their rust-red colour was still vivid.

My entire body shivered as the idea sank in that I was looking at real cave paintings left by real First Nations who lived a long time ago. Just how long ago I couldn't tell. "Who else knows about this?" I asked quietly.

"Well, let me see … there's me and then there's you. That makes two altogether."

"Are you serious? You mean no one else has any idea this place exists?" I murmured.

Louise nodded, then handed me her flashlight. I shone it from top to bottom and side to side. Not that I was any kind of expert in cave paintings, but some of the drawings appeared to be connected, as if they were telling a story or an event. There were lots of human figures, but in two distinct styles. One type had tiny bean-shaped heads, while the others had large heads with pointy chins.

"Do ya tink these guys are aliens?" Louise asked, indicating the figures with the pointed chins.

"Aliens?" I snickered. "That's some type of boat they're in, not a flying saucer."

"It must be a canoe," Louise said.

"Nah, I've never seen a canoe that long. Have you?" I asked aloud, though I was really talking to myself. "Those look like oars, not paddles." Next to the pointy-chinned people were lines with pointy tips shooting in two directions — like arrows.

"What do ya make of this picture — two humans, one big and the other small?" Louise asked.

"Could be a parent and child," I suggested.

"Maybe, but what's that? Some kind of animal?"

"It's got to be some kind of animal. I wonder why in the next picture it's lying beside one of the humans."

"Yah, and then in the final picture the little one's inside the boat again, like it's sailin' away."

"I don't know anything about the Beothuk people," I said.

"They died out after the Europeans and Mi'kmaq people pushed them out of their coastal territory. There's a story called *The Last Beothuk*."

"I remember learning that in school. Her name was Shanawdithit."

"That's right," Louise said. "She was the last known survivor of the Beothuks."

"Did they encounter the Vikings?"

"Oh, sure. The Vikings had a name fer them, too — skraelings. That's a Norse word for 'savage.'"

Louise and I sat quietly, thinking and observing. Finally, I asked, "How'd you find this place, Louise?"

"I was out scoutin' last week and saw a rabbit disappear into this hillside. I thought it was a warren and wondered if there were some babies inside. Instead of it being a small openin' fer rabbits I realized it was big enough fer me to fit through. I didn't have a flashlight, so I came back a few days later. That was the first time I saw the pictographs. When I heard ya were interested in archaeology, I knew I had to show ya … so ya can help me."

"Help you? To do what?"

"Help me study this place, of course. This is goin' to be the kind of thing that'll make us famous — like Louis and Mary Leakey. I bet they'll call me Louise Leakey — get it Louis, Louise?"

"Famous? Hmm." A little fame would be nice after all the rejection I'd had since coming to L'Anse aux Meadows. I pictured Robbie's face green with envy. Then, suddenly, my mind snapped back into shape as I heard my conscience calling me. It sounded an awful lot like a particular white-haired grandma known by some as Dr. Edwina McKay.

"This is an amazing place, Louise. I bet they'll want to name it after you — like Cave Louise or something. But we can't keep this to ourselves. It deserves experts, a plan, sophisticated technology, and we'll need to —"

"Blah-blah-blah. That's just the kind of thing Professor Brant would say. I never thought I'd get all that preachin' from someone my own age. I'm startin' to tink it was a big mistake to bring ya here."

Being compared to a stuffed shirt like Professor Brant was more than I could bear. "Yaow! Would you quit that? I'm nothing like Brant. I just think that —"

"They'll just take over and we'll have no part of it. Not only that, I guarantee they'll take all the credit fer findin' this place, too," Louise said, scowling.

"My friend Eddy's not like that. In fact, everything I know about archaeology and excavating she taught me. And thanks to her I've done lots."

"Lots?" Louise looked doubtful.

"Okay, three excavations, but that's not the point. Two kids — as brilliant as we might be — shouldn't just launch into an excavation without the help of someone who knows what they're doing. We could be responsible for losing important information."

I agreed with Louise that Professor Brant wasn't someone who would let a couple of kids be part of an important excavation. But Eddy wouldn't let him take this away from us. Would she?

"It's getting late, Louise. I say we sleep on it."

"Okay, but before we go there's something else ya should see. And I tink ya might finally agree this is too big to hand over to them bossy old folks."

She turned around and shone the flashlight at the base of the cave where there was a small indentation. At first it seemed like a pile of random hand-sized boulders, but when I looked closer I noticed the rocks were actually organized into a sort of tiny pyramid.

"Do ya know what it is?" Louise asked.

I got down on my haunches and studied the neat pile of stones. It only took a minute for the light to go on. "Holy crap! This is big, Louise. Really big!"

"Told ya, didn't I?" She smiled smugly.

"This rock cairn could be a burial marker. I read about them in —"

"*Dig* magazine? Yah, I read the same article. A little small fer a human burial, don't ya tink? On the other hand, maybe some ancient Beothuk buried his pet dog here." Louise howled at the idea.

"Right, like they really went to all this trouble to bury a dog." I was annoyed. "Louise, get a grip. Look around you. This place was made for a very specific reason. It was likely a sacred place to the early people. That's why they left all these pictures. They wanted to record their history or mark an important death." I could imagine a shaman standing in the same spot, performing a ritual. "This cairn might be marking someone's cremated remains ... or maybe it's a child's burial." We both fell silent and studied the cairn.

"Obviously, this is a sacred place," Louise said. "And I tink together we're capable of excavatin' this site by ourselves. Of course, we'll tell people about it once we've done the dig. We can even hand it over to the hob snobs from the field school if ya like, or to yer friend, Dr. McKay." Louise stood and pulled something from her pocket. "What we need are some photos of this place. Then I can upload them and see if I can learn something about their style and the meanin' of the images."

Before I had a chance to register what she was doing, she held up a camera and snapped a picture of the cave wall. "Stop!" I screeched at her.

She stepped back and scowled at me.

"The flash damages the pictographs. We need a low-light digital camera that won't harm the pigment in the paint."

"Fine, but ya don't have to yell! You're not goin' to turn all bossy on me, are ya?"

"I'm not trying to be bossy, Louise. But didn't you think about what kind of damage the flash would do? I mean, it's like basic Archaeology 101 stuff. C'mon, get with it."

Louise's face glistened pink. "Barney in the gift shop's a photographer. Maybe he'll have an idea where I can get a camera like that. Meanwhile, since you're so smart, ya can come up with the tools and a plan on how we're goin' to excavate this cairn." Louise turned so we were eye to eye. "Just remember — if those old fogeys from the field school find out about this place, it'll be off limits to us. Ya want that to happen?"

I looked at the cave paintings and the rock cairn. I wanted to excavate this site so bad my fingers ached. I knew Louise was right — no matter how fair Eddy was, Professor Brant was in charge and he'd never let us take part in the excavation. "Yah, my lips are sealed." At least for now, I said to myself.

"Aunt Gudrid, come quickly," Sigrid shouts from the doorway.

"What is it, girl? I'm boiling wool. What do you want?"

"It's Uncle's knarr — it's sailing into the bay. Come quickly. The men have returned from their Viking."

Gudrid throws the pail of water onto the fire. While it hisses and sends up a cloud of steam, she snaps up her little boy. "Come, Snorri, Fader is home."

News spreads quickly around the settlement, and everyone drops what they are doing to rush down to the shoreline. As the small band of Norsemen row their faering to shore, the settlers shout joyous greetings.

"Thank the gods, you have come home safely!" cries Gudrid.

Once he is on the shore, Thorfinn wraps his arms around his wife and laughs heartily. "And who do we have here?" he says as he scoops up his son. "Be this Snorri?" The child squirms and whines to be let down.

"Welcome, Uncle Thorfinn," Sigrid ventures shyly. "Snorri makes shy for a very short time. It won't last."

Her uncle's chest heaves. "There you are, my girl." Then

he steps back to look more carefully. "You seem matured since last I saw you. You're growing up on me. You look more like a woman than a maiden."

Sigrid's face turns crimson. "A shield maiden perhaps?"

Uncle Thorfinn laughs again, this time deep in the belly. "Are you still on about all that, my girl? I hoped you would be thinking of womanly things by now." He ruffles her hair and draws her in for a hug.

That night the house is filled with a warm glow from the fire and much merriment. Sigrid wishes there was fresh meat roasting on the spit instead of another pot of fish stew gurgling away in the cauldron. But no one else seems to mind. Instead everyone is intent on hearing about the men's adventures. But every story seems to take hours — for each man must tell it from his own experience.

"Everyone knows that a tale is but half told when only one person tells it," whispers Aunt Gudrid when Sigrid moans at hearing the same thing over and over.

When there is a lull in the conversation, Gudrid says, "Thorfinn, my husband, you have proved that he who has travelled far knows the ways of the world. Tell us what spirit governs the men you met. Were the skraelings you encountered as savage as the ones in this place?"

Uncle Thorfinn drags out a satchel and opens the string. Inside is some kind of vegetable. A ripple of murmurs spreads throughout the house as he sets them one at a time on the table. They are pale, like his wife's skin, and shaped like a bell. He takes his sword and slices through the thick outer shell. Inside, the hard flesh is bright orange and there is a pocket of seeds.

"We have no name for it, but the skraelings from the south grow them in abundance and call them askutasquash. They can be eaten raw, but I prefer them cooked. When we departed, they heaped bags upon us as a farewell gift. And not only these, they gave us grapes so sweet and plump they're like none you have ever seen or tasted. They'll make excellent mead."

"Skraelings who are hospitable — that is good," Gudrid announces.

"Yes, the southern skraelings are much less suspicious, and we traded successfully with them. They're eager for our metal tools, but I forbade the men to trade their swords or spears. Mainly, we traded furs for our red cloth and clay pots. Their leader urged us to stay longer so they could learn something about shipbuilding. But the journey south was difficult and dangerous, for we had to dodge many ice mountains floating in the water. I worried it could get worse on the return journey."

Soon the women pile hot fish stew onto the plates, and the tired travellers begin to eat. Sigrid looks for a chance to speak privately with her aunt.

"Are you going to tell Uncle about what happened to Snorri?" she whispers into her aunt's ear.

"Yes, I must," says Gudrid. Concern settles on Sigrid's brow. "But not tonight, daughter. I'll let him rest from his journey and then I'll tell him about what happened.

"Will he be very angry with me?" Sigrid asks.

Gudrid presses the girl's face between her hands. "Yes, I'm sure of it. But you're the light in his life, and I can't imagine he'll be angry for long. But know about it he must, for decisions need to be made."

"Decisions? Like what? Is there to be a *Thing*?" Sigrid knew if her aunt admitted there would be a council meeting, then the decision to be made was huge. What could it be? Whatever it was, it had something to do with her and what happened to Snorri.

"Whether Thorfinn calls for a *Thing* or not is no concern of yours, Sigrid. Now get yourself and Snorri off to bed. It's time for the adults to talk."

Sigrid finds sleep elusive. She cannot shake the feeling of dread over what her uncle will do when he learns about the disappearance of Snorri. Especially when he learns it was because she was practising sword fighting.

Before the cock crows, Sigrid slips out of bed and stumbles in the dark to the firepit. She stabs at the dying embers with a stick and then quickly adds firewood and fish oil to start a roaring fire. While she gazes into the bright flames, she notices that a familiar figure has moved beside her.

"Can't you sleep, Uncle?" asks Sigrid.

"No, Sigrid. But then again, no battle is won in bed."

Sigrid smiles at her uncle's funny saying. "Do you plan to battle today then?" she asks.

Thorfinn chuckles softly. "Not today, my girl," he whispers. "But one should always be ready."

Sigrid wonders if it would be in her favour if she were the one to tell her uncle about what happened. Perhaps it would soften his anger and lessen the punishment she was sure would follow.

"Uncle, while you were away ... I did something very bad."

"Oh? Tell me — what did you do?"

Sigrid can feel his eyes upon her. "Before I do, you should know that no one was harmed."

"I see. Go on then."

Sigrid takes a deep breath and launches into her story. She tells about coaxing Gunnar to take his grandfather's sword and meet her on the meadow to practise sword fighting. How she completely forgot about Snorri and did not even notice he had slipped away. Then the terror everyone felt as they searched, especially Aunt Gudrid. Sigrid decides to leave out the part about praying to Frigga and her dreadful promise to settle down and marry.

When her story is told, Thorfinn is quiet. Every moment he remains silent Sigrid grows more uncomfortable. She knows of people who were flogged for their failures, or worse — banished. Would her uncle do such a thing to her?

"Sigrid, your crime, as you've told it, is indeed quite serious," says Thorfinn slowly as he gazes into the flames.

While she waits for his next words, Sigrid feels her blood pump quickly through her veins.

Finally, Thorfinn looks up. "You know that from suffering comes wisdom."

"Yes, Uncle." So what suffering will her misdeed bring?

"I see you already suffer from fear about what will happen next."

"Yes, Uncle." Sigrid wrenches her fingers so hard they are numb.

"Would you say you're wiser for your suffering?"

"Yes, Uncle," Sigrid replies, fighting back tears.

"You've had your share of suffering in this life, perhaps more than most. But this suffering has given you an inner strength and wisdom."

"Yes, Uncle. But don't keep me in suspense any longer. What is to happen to me? What must be my punishment?"

"Put on your cloak, girl, and wait outside," Thorfinn commands.

Sigrid does as she is told. When Thorfinn comes out of the sod house, he is draped in his fur coat and carries his sword.

"Move along, girl. I want to get this over with before the clan wakes."

He guides Sigrid out to the meadow well beyond the settlement. Sigrid's body quakes, but she holds her head high, determined not to show her fear. A shield maiden would do the same, she thinks.

"This is far enough," Thorfinn tells her. Then he removes his cloak to reveal a second sword. "Here, take it."

Sigrid's hand trembles as she does as she is told. "I'm not afraid to die, Uncle."

"That is good." Thorfinn's face breaks into a grin that reaches from ear to ear, and he laughs deeply. "One day we all must die, but not today, my girl, not today."

"Why do you not seek revenge, Uncle?"

"Revenge? Sigrid, you're like my daughter. We're here so I can keep my promise to teach you sword fighting. I should have done it long ago. Now raise your blade, girl, raise it high."

Sigrid is flooded with joy, and she raises her sword. "Like this, Uncle?"

CHAPTER SEVEN

"Mornin', Princess." Waking to Bertha's voice was like being doused with a pail of cold water.

"Ahh, morning," I mumbled. "If it really is morning."

"Oh, it is. It's six o'clock. Time to get crackin', girl."

Yes, sir, Sergeant Bertha … hup-two-three-four. I rolled my legs over the side of the cot and shrieked when my toes touched the cold floor. "I didn't hear you come in last night," I said, buying myself some time to clear my mind.

"Couldn't sleep. I was agitated after His Highness dropped by, so I spent the night cleanin' and rearrangin' the kitchen from top to bottom. Then I went huntin' fer some new recipes. By the time I found some new things, it was nearly morning, so I put on a big pot of coffee and planned the meals fer today." She snapped her fingers in my face. "Now don't be fallin' asleep on me. See ya in the cook tent — ten minutes, missy."

When I stumbled into the kitchen thirteen minutes later, Bertha gave me the stink eye. She was already chopping up vegetables and had a large pot of water on the stove.

"I've been tinkin' — there's things we need to improve around here, things that'll make this a better camp kitchen. We can provide better service and food, speed up the process, and be more efficient."

"Hey, if it's efficiency you want, I have the perfect idea. It'll conserve energy and save money, too."

"I'm all ears," Bertha said. "Do tell."

I still didn't know her well enough to tell whether she was serious or just mocking me. "Say you want to make grilled cheese sandwiches. All you have to do is lay a bunch of bread or buns out on a buttered cookie sheet and cover them with sliced cheese. Then you take the cookie sheet and put it on the roof of the car — but you've got to make sure your car's been sitting in the full sun for a long time in order for this to work. Once you've done that, you let the sun melt the cheese from the top down while the hot metal of the roof cooks from below. You do the same for the tops, too. Might take half an hour — if it's a nice day — but you won't need a single volt of electricity." I waved my hands like a magician. "And, presto — grilled cheese. Well, more like solar cheese melt. Whatever you call it, it comes from free solar power."

Bertha looked at me stone-faced for a long time, didn't blink or budge or anything. Then her shoulders started to shake, her belly began to wobble, her mouth broke wide open, and out came a deafening explosion of laughter. Even worse — it went on and on for what felt like an hour. By the time she stopped, her cheeks were red and streaked with tears.

Annoyed, I said, "People laughed like that at Bell and Einstein, and Newton, too. But look where they ended up."

"Yes, they ended up in the same place we all do." Bertha snickered again, her jowls wiggling.

Really annoyed now, I said, "Laugh all you like. One

99

day people are going to be doing everything by solar power — even cook!"

"It's a terrific … *hee-hee* … idea, Princess. But what if … what if … *ohhh* … what if there's no sunshine? Or even worse … *snicker-snort* … ya don't have a car?" More howling, then finally she cleared her throat. "Solar cookin', eh? I'll definitely keep that one in mind."

After she wiped the tears from her cheeks a second time, she said, "Sorry, Princess, it must be the lack of sleep and too much caffeine. Now, where were we? Yah, ideas fer being more efficient — I was tinking of something less inventive."

"What if we take a poll of what the students and professors want to eat? That way they get what they want, less food is wasted, money is saved, and everyone's happy. I can get started on it right away," I offered.

"'Tis a good idea, fer sure. I got the same one last night and sent out my survey on the wireless. Got a bunch of texts and emails soon after. Seems these folks like their comfort foods — stews, shepherd's pies, soups, that sort of thing."

"So tell me again why we're having this conversation. You don't like my solar cooking idea, you already sent out a survey — why bother asking me when you've got this all figured out?"

"Now, now, Princess — no need to be so touchy. I just thought ya might want to add something." She turned on the stove and pulled out a mixing bowl. "Just so ya know, today's menu is pancakes fer breakfast, soup and grilled cheese fer lunch — done the old-fashioned way, of course — and fer dinner meat loaf and mashed potatoes."

"Great, carbs galore. That'll make them happy."

"Don't be cheeky with me, girlie. Now get yer hands washed. We've got lots of things to do."

The morning whizzed by, and I barely had time to stick my head out of the kitchen. Good thing, too, because I didn't know what I was going to tell Eddy when she asked why I'd missed the lecture. Until I figured that out, the best thing was to lie low.

After lunch was over, Bertha said, "You've done well today, Princess. I've got a proposition I tink you'll like. I need to leave ya on yer own while I make a trip to town. While I'm away, you'll peel those two bags of potatoes and then cook 'em up nice. If ya can handle that, I'll let ya off early today."

"Don't you need help with serving and cleaning up?" I asked, surprised.

Bertha smiled. "Got that covered. My daughter, Chloe, is comin' fer a visit and she loves to help me in the kitchen. It'll be a good time fer us to catch up. So what do ya say?"

"What do you think I'll say? Fantastic!" Getting off early would give me time to head back to the cave. I really wanted to see it again. I hoped by being there I'd get an idea how I could tell Eddy about it while at the same time ensure that Louise and I didn't lose out.

"All right, girlie, I'm off to the grocery store. Make sure ya don't let those potatoes burn or overcook. If ya do, I'll be boiling mad."

"Hmm … that's food for thought," I punned right back.

"Yah, it is, but don't ya make the mistake of tinkin' I don't mean it."

By the time I was into peeling my second sack of potatoes, my fingers were numb and shrivelled. After I washed the spuds, I popped them into the huge pot of boiling water. Taking Bertha's warning seriously, I hovered over the stove, stirring them every couple of minutes until they were finally done. We both had a lot at stake now. For Bertha it was her job and reputation, and for me, I wanted to be around long enough to excavate the cave site.

Draining off the water and getting the potatoes back into the pot was tricky. The pot and potatoes were really hot, and the steam scorched my hands and face. As I lifted the strainer to dump the heavy potatoes back into the pot, my wet hands lost hold of the handles. It was like one of those slow-motion moments as I watched the potatoes pour onto the floor.

I stared at the mess for a few seconds, wondering what I should do. There were no more potatoes, and even if there were, I didn't have the time, strength, or patience to peel even a single one. As I saw it, I had only one solution.

I dropped to the floor and started to scrape the potatoes back into the pot, at first with my bare hands. But they were so hot I had to grab a spoon to shove them back in. Then I quickly grabbed the mop and started cleaning up the mess on the floor. It was just a few moments later that I heard the screen door open, and there stood Bertha staring at me with eyes the size of eggs.

"I don't believe it," she pronounced. I stared back at her, silently panicking. "I tink I asked ya three times to wash that floor and ya pick this moment to finally do it? I'll never figure ya out, Princess. You're a real corker. Well, finish up and then come help me with the groceries."

Bertha turned around and went back out to the car. It wasn't until she was gone that I finally took a breath. As soon as my brain thawed, I quickly looked inside the pot. I had to pick out a few bits of dirt and other whatnots that had been taken up when I'd scraped the potatoes off the floor. After that I dumped the dirty wash water and rinsed off the mop.

Later I watched Bertha add fresh milk and butter to the pot. When she began whipping the potatoes with the electric mixer, I felt a little uneasy. Then I nearly gagged when she spooned out a sample and tasted it.

"Mmmm … they're perfect. Here, try it."

"Ah, no thanks. I'm not a big fan of mashed potatoes," I fibbed.

"Really? I don't tink I've ever met a kid who didn't like mashed potatoes. You're a strange one."

I didn't stick around to see what happened next, but I heard later that everyone heaped mashed potatoes onto their plates and not a scrap was left. Even Professor Brant enjoyed them so much he came back for seconds. And to think I'd nearly cooked my goose and fried my bacon. But lucky me … I managed to get out of that pickle!

Before hiking up to the cave I went to my tent and got a few things: my sketchbook, a flashlight, my jacket with a compass attached to the zipper, and my handy little tape measure — basic stuff for the on-the-go archaeologist.

I wanted to get a head start on some drawing and measuring of the site. I knew Louise wanted to keep the cave a secret — I couldn't blame her — but the little angels in my conscience were working overtime. On the one hand, it was an important site and who better to excavate it than Eddy? And who better to help her than me ... and Louise? But, on the other hand, Louise's fear that we'd get pushed out was legitimate. I hoped an idea would come while I was in the cave about what I should do.

It was only three-thirty, so there was a chance Eddy might spot me across L'Anse aux Meadows. Since I wasn't ready to talk to her, I needed to get past her and the students unseen. I made my way down Birchy Nuddick Trail and continued along the water's edge until I was far enough away. As I climbed the steep hillside, I checked regularly to make sure no one was watching me.

In the distance I saw the students practising excavation skills in a fake pit Professor Brant had made, complete with fake artifacts. I snickered at the idea. They were digging up plastic baubles while I was making my way to a real site — one that possessed incredible cave paintings and a rock cairn that was sure to have something crazy important buried underneath it.

The fire is burning bright, and Thorfinn is happy to be once again in the company of his family and friends. Just after he beats Ellandar at hnefatl for the third time, Gudrid puts her arms around him.

"Maybe you could put your board game away now. There might be someone who would enjoy a story," Gudrid says within earshot of Sigrid.

"Oh, I don't think there's anyone who cares to listen tonight," Uncle Thorfinn says, winking.

"Yes, there is. I'd like to hear a story, Uncle. Please tell a story," Sigrid pleads. "It's been so long."

"Well, there is one saga not often told, though it might be a bit frightening."

Sigrid's eyes open wide. "It won't frighten me." She looks around at the others. "Though maybe Gunnar will have to close his ears."

Uncle Thorfinn laughs. "All right, girl, you've been warned. Now it came to pass there was a fearless warrior by the name of Hervor and she was like no other."

Sigrid's eyes widen and she whispers, "Hervor was a shield maiden?"

Uncle Thorfinn nods. "Hervor's father and her mother's father were fierce and brutal warriors and were feared by all. So, as she grew older, few were surprised when Hervor refused to learn the skills of the women. Instead she took it upon herself to master the sword, the spear, and the bow, for she had every intention of becoming a warrior like her father."

"You do realize this will only fill her head with impossible ideas," hissed Gudrid. "Tell her a saga of Thor's adventures or the story of the giant Hymir — those are always entertaining."

"No, Uncle," Sigrid pleads. "Finish the story about Hervor."

Thorfinn averts his eyes from the glower upon his wife's face. "Now that I have started, I really should finish this story first." Gudrid shakes her head, clearly annoyed with her husband. "Now it may not surprise you that Hervor lacked all of the gentler qualities of her gender. Instead she honed her fighting skills on the boys and young men of her village, sending them home most days with terrible wounds and broken bones. Some say she was the most heartless female on Midgard and by far the most *beautiful of all women — with the exception, of course, of your Aunt Gudrid." As Thorfinn looks over at his wife, Sigrid glances at her cousin, Gunnar. She has been hard on him, too, sometimes, but she would never intentionally break his bones.*

"You said she was beautiful. What did she look like?" asks Sigrid.

"Legend says she had long, flowing hair — red like fire and gold like the sun."

"I have hair that colour, too," Sigrid says, smiling.

Gudrid thumps around the house, grumbling. "Someone is going to regret this," she promises.

"Yes, you do have hair the same as Hervor, but that's where the similarities end, Sigrid. While you're as brave, for sure, you'll never be so cruel. You see, Hervor became one of the most feared and brutal raiders who ever lived. When she faced her foe, she didn't just run them through, as did other warriors. She fought like a berserker and took pleasure in gutting her enemy from head to groin. Perhaps it was the spell of Tryfing — the sword she ripped from the hands of her dead father.

"Tryfing was made by the dwarfs of Dvallin and Durin. It was Odin's grandson, Svafrlami, who trapped them. They were forced to forge the sword. It had a hilt made of solid gold and possessed immense power. It is said that with Tryfing in hand its owner always struck down his opponent and could even cut through metal and stone. But the sword was possessed with an evil that infected anyone who owned it. Each time it was drawn someone was sure to die ... and at the same time its owner went a little more insane.

"In time Hervor became known far and wide. She even found her way to the court of a great king. Perhaps it was out of fear that he invited her to be his guest. While they were engaged in a game of hnefatl, one of the king's men made the poor decision to touch Tryfing. It took only a moment for Hervor to notice the indiscretion and leap into action. She snatched her sword and —" Thorfinn's story comes to an abrupt end when Snorri pushes past the listeners and climbs into his father's arms.

"Fader," the boy says. "I talk, I talk." He looks at the others, smiles, then babbles some more words no one can understand. Everyone finds his antics amusing except Sigrid.

"Snorri," she growls, "let Uncle finish his story. Go on, Uncle. Tell us what happened."

Her edgy words make Snorri all the more determined to hold the audience's attention. He kicks his feet and buries his head in his father's shoulder, crying, "I talk, I talk." Sigrid lifts her hand to pull the child from his father's knee when Gudrid steps in.

"Sigrid," she says sharply. "Don't forget, he, too, missed his father and wants a little attention." Right on cue, Snorri smiles up at Thorfinn and utters more babble.

"I'll finish the story later," Sigrid's uncle promises.

"Fine." Sigrid takes her leave and storms to the farthest end of the house. Soon after the rest of the group breaks up and goes off to other activities.

I will never be as wicked as Hervor, *Sigrid thinks.* But I shall master the sword, and after that it will be the spear and the axe. *She knows better than to make her ambitions known, especially to Aunt Gudrid. But she cannot help but dream that one day her name, too, will be a legend and children will speak of her.* What will they call me? *she wonders.* How about Sigrid the Fearless?

Suddenly, she remembers her promise to Frigga.

"Uncle, I have a confession to make," *says Sigrid a while later when Snorri is fast asleep on his lap.*

"Another confession? I don't think I can manage another one." *Uncle Thorfinn sees that his niece is determined.* "All right then, tell me. What have you done now?"

"I made a promise."

"Yes, go on."

"It was a silly promise, really. And I made it out of fear when I thought Snorri was lost. But now I want to take it back."

"I see. And to whom did you make the promise?"

"Frigga," *Sigrid says timidly.*

Thorfinn is quiet for what feels like an eternity. Then finally he says, "Once you make a promise, especially to Frigga, you can't go back on your word. It would be dishonourable."

Sigrid's heart feels as if it will break. "But, Uncle, I promised her I would marry that wrinkled old trader, Bjorni, if she kept Snorri safe. I also promised I would give up my dream to be a shield maiden and instead become a normal wife and mother. But I simply can't do it."

"And why not? Bjorni is a perfectly good match ... and wealthy, too."

"If I marry him, our children will be homelier than dwarfs from the underworld. And secondly, I would rather die than marry that old man."

Thorfinn stares for a long time at this most peculiar girl. Soon his shoulders and belly begin to tremble. Then out of his mouth pours laughter so loud that Thor and Odin must think a thunderstorm rages in Midgard.

"And if you're not to marry old Bjorni — who, I might add, is younger than me — then who will you marry?" Thorfinn wipes tears of hilarity from his eyes. "Do you think it will be easy for me to find a man who will take such an impudent and overbearing girl such as you?"

"Easy or difficult — it makes no difference to me, for I don't want the life of a wife and mother. I will be a warrior." Sigrid folds her arms defiantly to show she is serious.

Thorfinn smiles at her, perhaps realizing for the first time that his beloved Sigrid is no longer a child. "The way of the Norsemen is changing, Sigrid. We are becoming peaceful and settled. There are not so many who want to pillage and battle anymore. And with fewer battles there isn't the need for so many warriors."

"Maybe so, but, Uncle, we'll always need defending against the skraelings."

Uncle Thorfinn is quiet as he contemplates his next words. "You're correct about the skraelings, Sigrid. If we stay here, we'll always need warriors to defend the settlement. But many of the elders feel these wild ones will never let us alone. They're stealthy and unshakable. And what happened to Snorri was a warning to us. There are many in the community who don't feel the danger is equal to the fortune this place has to offer. Tonight we shall hold a Thing to discuss it."

Sigrid juts her chin out defiantly. "What does it matter what they say, Uncle Thorfinn? You're the leader. You'll just have to tell them this is where we live. And they shouldn't worry, for I'll be ready to defend them."

"It's not so simple, Sigrid. Yes, I'm the head of our tribe, but I must consider the wishes of the others. And a decision will be made at tonight's Thing."

"A decision? A decision about whether we're to stay or leave?"

"Yes, Sigrid. Most of the men want to leave this place to the skraelings and make ready to return to our homeland. And I do, too."

Sigrid is stunned by this news. If she returns home, it most certainly means the end of her dream to be a shield maiden.

The day before, I had tagged the cave entrance with a blue cord off my sweater. The cave was so well disguised that if I hadn't, I might not have found it again on my own. I'd thought about the cave and its paintings all day and was excited to go inside and see them again. I switched on my flashlight and slowly made my way through the narrow entrance. Inside, the air was still and cool and had an earthy scent. It was quiet, too — maybe even a bit eerie.

The idea slowly dawned on me that nobody knew where I'd gone. I could hear Aunt Margaret in the back of my mind nattering at me: *Peggy, you never think before you leap.* She was right, if something were to happen to me ... "Oh, Peggy, shut up!" I told myself before my imagination got away on me.

Still, there was no getting around the fact that I was alone in a cave that only I and one other person knew about. And if I was alone, why did I have the feeling of being watched?

I set down my backpack and shone the light onto the cave walls. As it penetrated the cracks and crevices and lit up the paintings, I started to feel more at ease. The pictures were simple but had an artistic elegance about them. Many of the figures were animals. I wasn't sure, but they looked like caribou, foxes, fish, and seals. Others were humans — I could tell that much. But why did some have pointed chins and others didn't?

I read once that early people used fish eggs mixed with red ochre — iron oxide deposits from the earth — to make paint and usually applied it by hand. I let my fingers lightly trace the red lines of the pictures and noticed they were about the same thickness. With just a bit of imagination I pictured the cave lit by firelight and a Beothuk, maybe a shaman, dipping his fingers into a shell filled with the mixture and then applying it to the cave wall.

I took out my sketchpad. I wanted to capture the images so I could study them later. Shading and smudging, I did my best to make my drawings look as elegant as the originals. Soon I was lost in thought as I filled page after page. Since there was no natural light in the cave, I didn't have a clue how much time had passed. Neither did I realize the batteries in my flashlight had worn down — not until I suddenly found myself in total darkness.

The moment the light went out I gasped at the utter blackness. I'd never known what total darkness was really like before. I couldn't even see my hand in front of my face. While it was fascinating, it was also a whole new level of freaky.

I admit that my heart was beating so fast that it started pulsating in my ear. I almost thought it was coming from the cave and not me. Before I hit the panic button I gave myself a pep talk. "Okay, Peggy, don't freak out. Everything is going to be fine. You just have to find your way to the cave wall and follow it to the entrance." I felt around for my backpack, slid my sketchpad and pencil inside, and zipped it up tight.

Crawling for what seemed like forever, I finally felt the cold, hard wall. Slowly, I stood, careful not to bump my head. Then I shuffled toward where I thought the cave entrance was located. My hand brushed against something wet and slimy — and I admit, I shrieked. "Calm down, Peggy. All you've got to do is get yourself to the entrance where there's sure to be beams of light coming from outside."

No sooner had the words come out of my mouth than I tripped. Reaching out for something to hold on to, I found only air and fell onto a heap of rocks. Suddenly, I was in a lot of pain. I'd cut myself and was bleeding badly. It was all I could do not to bawl like a baby.

As I lay there wondering what to do, I heard scraping noises. I couldn't see a thing — no matter how wide open my eyes were — but I was sure something was coming through the cave entrance. Was this how it was to end — supper for a hungry wolf?

Then the cave was flooded with light.

"I was afraid I'd find ya here," said Louise, sighing.

"I'm so glad to see you," I nearly sobbed, then quickly noticed she wasn't nearly as relieved to see me as I was to see her.

"Do ya realize they're all out lookin' fer ya?" she said crossly.

"Who's looking for me? What are you talking about?"

"It's nearly nine o'clock and dark, Peggy."

"It is? I had no —"

"You've been away fer so long that friend of yers — the old lady —"

"Eddy?"

"Yah, that one. She formed a search party, and they're all lookin' fer ya now. She tracked me down at home and asked me if I knew where ya might have gone. I had to lie on the spot, and I'm not so good at that. What were ya tinkin' comin' here alone?"

"You come here alone," I defended.

"Yah, but I'm a local. You're an outsider and a kid at that. People don't take it well when a kid disappears." Louise waved her hand. "C'mon, let's get goin'. I just hope no one saw me come here."

As if on cue, a voice came through the cave entrance. "Hello, is someone in there?"

Louise held her finger to her lips and switched off the light. I froze, too, when I recognized the voice.

"If you kids are in there, you'd better speak up now."

I wanted to say something, but I could feel Louise squeeze my arm. Then came the sounds of grunting and scraping and finally the beam from a flashlight was glaring in my eyes.

"Peggy! Thank goodness!" Eddy puffed. "My dear, you're bleeding."

When my eyes adjusted to the light, I looked down and saw my sleeves were as red as the paint on the walls.

"And, Louise, I figured you knew something. That's why I followed you. For the record, Peggy would never go off to town to get her nails done. Nor would she slink off to some private place to read a romance novel."

I frowned and glanced at Louise.

She glared back. "I told ya I don't lie well when put on the spot. And tanks to you the cat's out of the bag." For once I had nothing to say. "And by the way — good job on the rock cairn. Ya saved us all the effort of dismantlin' it carefully."

"Wha-what?" I stuttered, looking down at where I had fallen. The stones that had once formed a small rock cairn were now a messed-up pile of rocks. *"Noooo!"* I cried out loud.

Eddy shone her flashlight at the messed-up cairn, back to me for a second, and then beamed her light onto the cave wall. I watched her shudder. "Oh, my goodness," she said in a hushed voice. It was nearly the same reaction I'd had when I saw the cave paintings for the first time. All three of us stood in silence.

Then Eddy glanced at me. I felt as if I would shrivel up on the spot. Now I knew what people meant when they said, "If looks could kill."

"I wanted to —"

"Save it, Peggy. We need to get you out of here and back to camp where we can tend to those wounds," Eddy said. Her voice wasn't angry — more like she was regretful. "Besides, there are a lot of people who will want to know that you're safe."

I somehow doubted that.

Louise grabbed my pack. "C'mon, ya heard her."

As I followed them out of the cave, I turned back to see the pictographs one last time. I was pretty sure I'd never see them again.

CHAPTER EIGHT

"There's no use arguin' the matter, Princess. Ya were in the wrong, and now you're payin' the price. Don't be tinkin' I'm glad about it, either. Now, instead of ya bein' my helper, I've got to be yer babysitter." Bertha set down a tray of eggs. "Now get crackin'. We're havin' French toast fer breakfast — and there'll be none of yer funny business. Just follow the recipe."

I didn't have much to say, so I grabbed the eggs and bowl and started preparing the egg mixture. Try as I might, I couldn't stop having flashbacks about the night before.

When we got back to L'Anse aux Meadows, Eddy took me to the cook tent where she'd set up an emergency search headquarters. That was when I had to face all the students and professors who had been out looking for me. While Eddy attended to my cuts, Professor Brant raked me over the coals for putting myself in danger and inconveniencing everyone else. That was humiliating enough, but what was worse was how he lit into Eddy.

"Dr. McKay, I'm very disappointed in you. After all, hiring this girl was your idea. She's a terrible cook's assistant and has no common sense, either. The entire evening was wasted because we had to search for her when our first obligation was to these students."

I hated to see Eddy being talked to like that. But the professor was right. She should have known better than to let me come.

After Professor Brant was finished his performance, the students left for their own tents. It wasn't until then that Eddy told him about the cave. Anyone else would have been happy about it, but not him.

"Is this true? And you didn't tell us about it? All I can say is you better not have done anything to disturb the site."

Louise had gone home, so I figured I was getting her share of the blame, too. I was surprised that Eddy didn't say anything about how I'd knocked over the cairn.

When I was finally allowed to go to bed, I arrived to find Bertha sound asleep and there was already a parade of noises coming out of both ends of her. In a strange way it was comforting. I mean, I couldn't exactly sleep, anyway. Better to listen to Bertha's butt than the noise in my head.

That next morning, when the students began filing into the cook tent, it was clear the word was out about the cave and the place was humming with excitement. I knew that I'd be banned from going anywhere near it. Now I could only hope to overhear tidbits of information during meals.

Eddy didn't show up for breakfast, so I got worried. When Robbie came to get seconds on French toast, I asked about her. Any hope that she'd take pity on me was dashed by the look on her face.

"Stop talking to me, kid. People might think we're friends." That went right to the heart.

"Now that wasn't a nice thing to say even if ya did make a big mistake," said Bertha after Robbie was gone.

"I just want to know if Eddy's all right," I said quietly.

Later that morning Bertha brought me news about Eddy. "She's takin' her meals at the cave site today. Apparently, she's got a lot to do — something about doing a site assessment and then creatin' an excavation plan. But don't feel too bad. Only a few of the students get to help her."

Was she kidding? Don't feel bad? It should be Louise and me helping Eddy.

For the next couple of days Bertha kept me on a short leash. The only news I got was what I overheard at mealtime. When Bertha got sick of having me underfoot, she said I could wander around L'Anse aux Meadows as long as I stayed far from the field school students and the cave. By then everyone knew me and what I looked like, so there was no chance I'd sneak up for a peek without some kind of intervention.

I drifted into the settlement where lots of tourists were enjoying the Viking guides and sod buildings.

"My husband's a saga freak and we've visited all the important Viking sites in Norway, Denmark, Iceland, Greenland, even the Faroe Islands," a lady was telling John.

I waved at him as I passed by and heard him say, "With all yer travellin' I bet you've never heard how the Vikings were able to make fire when they were out at sea." Then he began telling the tourists about the stinky pee-soaked fungus mats the Vikings used to take fire with them. I snickered when someone shrieked in disgust.

I wondered if I'd see Louise around. We hadn't had a chance to talk since the night Eddy had found us in the cave. She was probably feeling as miserable as me. When the crowd cleared off, I'd see if she was in the longhouse.

When I heard a clanking noise, I followed it to the forge. A man with long silver hair tied back was forging a metal nail. I was the only one there to watch him heat the iron until it was nearly white-hot, then use some kind of ancient pliers to shape it. It took him quite a while to make that one nail. Finally, he dipped it into a pail of cold water and it hissed as it cooled down.

"Here, a present fer the young lady."

I took it in my hand, noticing it was still warm. "Thank you," I said, admiring how something as simple as a nail could be so much work to make.

"You're awfully young to have such a long face," he said. "What's yer problem?"

He was a kind-looking man, but I didn't feel like spilling my guts about what was bugging me to a stranger. "It's a long story, but the short version is I made a real mess of things and now my best friend's reputation is ruined."

"I see. Well, at least ya haven't had to face the pole of scorn."

"Pole of scorn? What's that?" I asked.

"To the Vikings, a man's reputation and honour during his life determined his fortune after death. Any offence in word or deed, or anything that might mar his reputation or honour, had to be avenged. It was the only way to repair the wrong. Sometimes it was a duel, or the one wronged had to hurt the other equally or worse. But sometimes the wronged man erected a pole of scorn with carvings of the wrongdoer's head and a curse in runes along the pole. One such fellow by the name of Jokull killed the mare of his wrongdoer and mounted it on the pole, too."

"Nasty!"

"Quite nasty, indeed. But the Norsemen were a sensitive lot and tolerated no threat against their name and person. But I doubt yer misdeed was so bad ya deserved the pole of scorn."

"It's kind of a long story, and I don't really feel like talking about it."

"That's a pity, fer I love a good story." He patted the seat beside him, encouraging me to sit. "Maybe ya don't care to tell yer story, but how do ya feel about hearin' one? I've got ones that'll make ya laugh and others that'll curl yer hair."

I sat next to the man. "Sure, I could use the distraction."

"Well, good. What's yer name, girl?"

"Peggy."

"That's a good name. I'm Niko Ekstrom."

"Hey, you're the expert on Viking sagas," I observed.

He chuckled. "I suppose some call me an expert. After a lifetime learnin' about the Norse, it's more like an obsession. My wife, Ava, says it's a curse. Instead of bein' called a saga expert I prefer the title storyteller. If I'd been around in the old days, people would've paid me to recite the sagas of the gods and heroes, or tell about the great battles and family feuds."

"How about stories about Leif Eriksson and how he and his men came to North America?"

"Sure, there's lots of stories about Lucky Leif. But which of the stories is true isn't so easy to tell," Niko explained.

"There are two versions of the Vinland Sagas. One is called *Saga of the Greenlanders* and the other *Saga of Erik the Red*. In one Leif is credited with all the glory fer discoverin' Vinland, and in the other his role is played down and Thorfinn Karlsefni and his wife, Gudrid, are the heroes."

I'd learned about Leif Eriksson in school, but I'd never heard about the other guy before.

"She wants to hear stories about the shield maidens, Niko. That's what she's really interested in."

I turned to see Louise in her Viking costume. She smiled at me.

"Shield maidens? Well, then fer sure you'll be wantin' to hear about Thorfinn Karlsefni. He sailed here with three ships and about a hundred and fifty men, a handful of women, and some young folk, too. We know from the sagas that Gudrid gave birth right here to her first child, a lad they called Snorri. He became the first European born in North America."

"Snorri?" I snickered. "That's even worse than my friend's name — Thorbert."

"Why Thorbert's a perfectly respectable name. Don't you agree, Miss Runa?"

Louise shrugged. "If you're a Viking. If you're a kid from the twenty-first century, it's like wearin' a sign — DORK HERE."

"So you know stories about shield maidens?" I asked, changing the subject. "I'd like to hear some."

"The first thing ya have to understand is how the Norsemen mixed their myths and history together in the sagas. Scholars have been tryin' to unravel fact from fiction fer centuries."

"Were shield maidens fiction?"

"No, I tink there really were some female warriors, though some scholars tink they were only Norse fantasy. Have ya heard about Hervor and Brynhildr?" I shook my head. "In that case ya fer sure won't know about a young warrior who came to this very settlement with Karlsefni and his crew. In the stories she was known as Sigrid the Brave. Like all shield maidens, she rejected the traditional role and expectation of young women of her time. She refused to learn to cook or weave and showed no desire to be a wife or mother. Then along came baby Snorri, and despite her objections, Sigrid became his main caregiver. In fact, it was while he was in her care that she earned the name Sigrid the Brave."

"Sounds like my kind of girl. Will you tell us about her?" I asked.

Old Niko smiled. "There's an old Norse saying — 'A man listens thus he learns.' So make yerself comfortable, girls, and I'll tell ya all about the brave young Sigrid."

I scooted over, and Louise sat next to me. Then Niko began. His voice was just how a storyteller's should be — deep and soothing. I could feel him take us into the past to a time long ago.

"Now it came to pass that there was a young orphan girl by the name of Sigrid Thorbjornsdottir …"

As soon as Sigrid hears Snorri's gentle, rhythmic breathing, she slips out of the bed and tucks him in tightly. When she is sure he is fast asleep, she sneaks out of the longhouse and slyly makes her way to the firepit. Hiding in the shadow of the forge, she has a perfect view of the lively meeting. As chief, Uncle Thorfinn sits prominently on his chair while the men debate the issue at hand. Aunt Gudrid sits at his side. To some she might appear calm, but Sigrid notices she is wringing her hands.

"It is too soon to give up on the venture, Thorfinn," booms Ellandar. "If we're the kind of men who could be frightened by some wild-haired skraelings, we would never have left Greenland in the first place."

"It doesn't make a man a coward to respect his opponent. These savages may be wild, but they're stealthy," argues Ingerson. "And if they're so harmless, why do you sleep so lightly at night? Could it be that you're like the rest of us and don't want to die in your sleep?" Many on both sides of the issue groan or grumble.

Uncle Thorfinn interjects. "Come now, Ingerson, we all know it isn't a question of whether we die here or die at home. The important thing is to live and die in honour. Now don't question Ellandar's courage. Stick to the issue. Everyone can see that the best lumber has been depleted already, and over the past two years the hunting has become more difficult with fewer game animals around."

As she watches, Sigrid's chest heaves with pride. Her uncle is a wise man and speaks confidently. That is why the other men listen.

"Ouch!" she cries out when something hard hits her head. Fortunately, the debate is now lively and no one hears her.

"Shh," Gunnar whispers. "What do you think Thorfinn will do if he catches you here?" He sidles up to his cousin.

"You brat. What did you throw at my head?"

Gunnar bends down and picks up a piece of slag left from the day's forging.

She snatches it from his fingers and flicks it at him. "Now shut up. I'm trying to hear the debate. They may be close to a decision."

"My father says there's no way a hundred and fifty Norsemen will come to an agreement in one night."

"Then, if he must, Uncle Thorfinn will decide the matter. He's the leader, after all — hand-picked by Erik the Red himself."

"We all know what Thorfinn wants to do — he'd have us tuck our tails like frightened dogs and let the skraelings have this land."

"Careful with your words, Gunnar. You already know I can best you with the sword and in arm wrestling. Want to find out what I can do with my knuckles?"

Gunnar frowns. "You know, one day I'll be a full-grown man. I'd like to see you take me then."

Sigrid leaps onto her cousin and pins him to the ground. "Do you think I want to return to Greenland? I assure you, nothing awaits me there but a very old man who wants me for his bride. But Uncle Thorfinn is wise, and if he says we must leave, then so be it." She frees the boy and sits on the ground next to him. "He says our best chance to get home before winter sets in means we'll have to leave within the next two fimmts, perhaps on Odin's day or Thor's day."

As the two watch silently from their hiding place, Sigrid cannot help think what her future offers. Her uncle said that the ways of the Norsemen have changed and many warriors had turned their hand to farming instead. If there is no chance for her to fight in battles, then what is left for the likes of her?

The Thing drags on, and Gunnar loses interest. After he slips away to his warm bed, Sigrid decides she, too, has had enough of hiding in the shadows. She will learn what is to happen soon enough, she thinks, and steals back to the longhouse. Sigrid is chilled and would like to crawl in beside Snorri. But after a quick feel of his damp bed she changes her mind and slides into her own bed instead without a bit of guilt. Let Aunt Gudrid clean him for once, she thinks as she drifts off to sleep.

Long after the cock crows the settlers sleep on. Sigrid can feel that the morning is wearing on by the cracks of light that seep through the chinks in the sod house. Soon she hears the banging of pots as Aunt Gudrid makes ready the morning meal.

"What was decided last night?" Sigrid asks while her aunt heats the fish stew.

"I thought you knew? You were spying, weren't you?"

Sigrid's face feels warm. "Spying? I, ah … well, maybe just a little. Gunnar was, too. But I couldn't stay until the end."

Sigrid notices for the first time that Gudrid looks almost happy. "We're leaving soon, girl, and there's much to do in preparation. We must start right away, and every-one will need to help."

Sigrid feels numb and flops onto the bench.

"We've all been assigned jobs. You're to boil and pre-pare the fungus mats," says Gudrid.

Suddenly wide awake, Sigrid howls, "Me? Why me? That's the most disgusting job in the world. I don't want to stand over a stinking pot of Norsemen urine. I'd rather die at the hand of an ogre."

"I thought you might feel that way. But since dying isn't an option, you'll be in charge of the fungus mats. You're always saying you don't like women's work, so there you have it." Gudrid can barely conceal her glee. For once she has the upper hand.

"Perhaps I should watch over Snorri instead and let you do that work. After all, I'm just a girl. I can help dry the fish and collect firewood, too."

Gudrid snickers into her apron.

"Thanks, Niko. I really enjoyed hearing about Sigrid the Brave," I said when Niko's story came to an end. "It's really cool the way the Beothuk tried to help her."

"Yah, the settlers realized this the moment they found the bear's body riddled with arrowheads. Then they realized the arrow points were made from discarded iron slag and spent iron nails from behind the forge. It was most unsettlin'," said Niko.

"Is that because it showed the Beothuk were capable of sneaking into their village?" asked Louise.

"Exactly. It showed the Norsemen the potential danger they faced as long as the two were enemies."

It was time I went back to the cook tent. I was already in the doghouse with too many people. I couldn't risk being late and upsetting Bertha again. "Thanks, Niko. Can I come again and hear more stories?"

"Absolutely, Peggy. It's what I do."

Louise followed me when I left. "So when are the hob snobs goin' to let us help with the excavation?"

There wasn't an easy way to say this. "Ah, well … I don't … I mean, it doesn't seem …"

"I knew it. They're not goin' to let us, are they? I told ya this would happen," Louise growled. I could see her anger simmering. "That's my cave, you know. I found it. So what about that friend of yers? I thought ya said she wasn't like the others."

"She's not, Louise. But Professor Brant has it in for her now, too. I don't think she has any say in the matter."

Louise growled some more. "What a big mistake it was to let ya see my cave. Now look where it's got me."

"I'd probably feel the same way, but I still think it's better that the cave is going to get the kind of expert treatment it deserves. There's no arguing that it's going to be one of the most important sites in eastern Canada. They'll probably make a documentary about it and show it on the History Channel."

"Really? And who do ya think will get all the credit fer discoverin' it?" Louise's eyebrows were furrowed deeply. "Ya know, it isn't so much that they're goin' to get all the credit. What hurts more is that they won't even let me be part of the excavation."

Louise was right. It was bad enough I'd been banned, but they didn't need to punish her, too. If she hadn't been curious and made the discovery, they'd still be digging in a pretend excavation site with Tinkertoys and other junk in place of real artifacts.

"If I can, I'll try to talk to Eddy, okay? I know they'll never let me, but maybe she can find a way for you to get in there." When we parted, Louise looked a tiny bit hopeful.

After I got back to the cook tent, Bertha had already cooked the noodles for the lasagna. "Good, just in time to do the layerin'," she said. "I've got to start on the pies."

As I worked, I played over in my mind the story Niko had told about Sigrid the Brave. She was definitely my kind of girl. When I accidently poured tomato sauce onto my shirt, it made me think about Sigrid's blood-stained tunic and how her life had ended. Then there was me — destined to die of boredom.

"Hi, Peggy," Eddy said when she came in for supper. My face flushed, and I tried to avoid eye contact. "I thought you might want to eat your supper with me."

I looked over at the tables of students and the other professors and knew what their reaction would be if I was to pull up a seat with them all.

"I meant just the two of us. I thought you'd like to hear what's been happening."

"Thanks, Eddy, I'd like that. But I don't know if Bertha will —"

"If Bertha will what? I'm not the ogre's wife, ya know. Ya have to eat, after all. Ya might as well do it with yer friend." Bertha smiled as she held out a tray to me. "Well … go on then."

"How have you been holding out?" Eddy asked after we tucked ourselves at a table far from the crowd.

I shrugged. "Oh, you know — hunky-dory, peachy-keen, A-okay. And despite Bertha's best efforts, I'm still not a very good cook." I fiddled with my food while trying to think of the words I needed to say. "I hope you know how sorry I am about all the trouble I've caused you, Eddy. And I hope you believed me when I said I wanted to tell you all about the cave when I first learned about it. That day I went there, I was hoping to figure out how to honour Louise's wish while also letting you know about it. I would have told —"

"Peggy, I know you have a good head on your shoulders. That's all water under the bridge now."

I thought about what Niko had said about the pole of scorn and was glad Eddy wasn't a Viking and that vengeance wasn't her style.

"Don't you want to hear what's going on at the cave site?" Eddy asked.

"You know I do," I protested. "It's been on my mind practically non-stop."

"It's incredible. I've never seen a cave like it. The pictographs alone will keep some lucky archaeologist busy for years. Then there are the artifacts littered throughout the cave. You probably didn't see them because it was too dark. And, of course, there's the rock cairn, too."

"Did you begin excavating it?" I asked anxiously.

"That's what I wanted to talk to you about. It's amazing and yet puzzling, too."

"What's amazing and puzzling?" I asked impatiently.

"We don't understand what it means yet. And maybe we never will."

"Are you trying to drive me out of my mind? What's so amazing and puzzling, Eddy?"

She laughed. "Some things never change. Okay, when we removed the pile of rocks we found —" she bent closer to me as if she were telling a secret "— a huge animal skull. We think it's a bear, but we're not certain. We have a zooarchaeologist coming tomorrow to help us identify it."

"A zooarchaeologist?"

"Yes, an archaeologist who specializes in animal remains and how they relate to human activity."

"So this person is going to be able to determine what kind of animal it is?"

"Yes, and most likely tell us the exact species, something about how the head was severed from the animal's body, the age of the animal, maybe a cause of death — all sorts of things, I imagine."

"Maybe the Beothuk worshipped bears. Or maybe they were honouring it after they killed it for its fur," I said.

"Those are good suggestions for why they might have buried an animal's skull in what was clearly a very sacred place. The cave paintings seem related, too. But I'm glad the zooarchaeologist is coming. She'll be able to help us solve some of this. I'll keep you posted."

I was totally bummed out and excited at the same time. What I wouldn't give to be at the site the next day. "Thanks, Eddy. I appreciate hearing the news. No one else will even speak to me, let alone give me any information. So I'm glad things between us are good."

"You're a good kid, Peggy. Impulsive and misguided at times, but I know you care and would always try to do what's best for the protection of the site. And when the others take the time to get to know you, they'll see that, too."

Then I remembered Louise. "You know, none of this would be going on if it wasn't for Louise. If she hadn't found the cave, who knows if or when it would have been discovered. It's not fair that she's not allowed to be part of this excavation."

"I know what you mean. And I agree she hasn't been given the recognition she deserves. I'll put a good word in but can't promise anything. After all, my name is mud, too."

Knowing that Eddy's reputation was marred because of me made my heart ache. "I'm sorry, Eddy. I know that's my fault."

"No hard feelings. Do you think this is the first time I've been in hot water? Why, I've probably been in more trouble than you ever will."

Now that seemed hard to believe. "Really? You always know what the right thing is to do."

"Sure … now, but I was young once … and impulsive, lacked judgment, and got into plenty of trouble. Seems for some of us it's the way we learn." Eddy smiled and ruffled my hair.

That night I fell into bed and dropped off to sleep without any trouble. Even Bertha and all her noises didn't bother me. It definitely helped hearing about what was going on at the site, but mostly I was happy knowing Eddy and I were still good friends.

CHAPTER NINE

I'd been at L'Anse aux Meadows for two weeks. In that time I'd managed to turn the entire archaeology field school against me, botch a lot of meals and jeopardize Bertha's job, get Louise banned from the cave she'd found, and ruin Eddy's good reputation.

I came to Newfoundland thinking I'd be her teaching assistant and take part in an excavation. Instead I'd been banned from getting anywhere near the field school, the students, and the cave site. On top of that I was now Bertha's kitchen elf, allowed out only when every pot was washed and the next meal prepared. The only thing I had to look forward to was news from Eddy about the cave excavation. Beyond that, my only goal was to stay out of further trouble.

At lunchime that day Eddy said, "Peggy, this is Dr. Natasha Soleil. She's the expert in animal remains I told you about."

"You're a zooarchaeologist, right?" I hoped I'd said it right.

"Yes, I am. And you, I hear, plan to be an archaeologist, too, one day. What area do you think you'll specialize in?" Dr. Soleil asked.

"I want to be an osteologist, like Eddy."

Eddy smiled. "You might change your mind when you get older. Perhaps you'll find animal bones more to your liking — learning how early people used them for tools and weapons and how they harvested them. I know I've learned a lot from Dr. Soleil already."

"About the skull you found in the cave?" I asked.

"Yes," Eddy said. "She not only confirmed it's a bear skull, but more specifically it's a polar bear."

"And clearly the associated arrowheads show the animal died a violent death," added Dr. Soleil. "Those arrowheads raise many questions, too."

"That's right," Eddy said. "Traditionally, the Beothuk used flint, obsidian, or sometimes bone. But the arrows in this burial are iron. So either this bear was killed by the Norsemen or the Beothuks traded for the iron. Either way, the severed bear skull must have had special significance to have been given a ritual-like burial in a cave full of pictographs."

That was pretty incredible stuff. "So does it look like they were —" Just then I felt a very annoying tap on my shoulder. When I turned around, I saw Bertha glaring at me.

"How's about ya wrap this little chit-chat up?" Bertha pointed to the line of people behind Eddy and Dr. Soleil waiting to get their lunch.

"Oh, yes. So sorry," said Eddy. "We'll find time later to fill you in more, Peggy." They both helped themselves to quiche as I poured their corn chowder. "It looks delicious — bet I've put on five pounds since I arrived." As Eddy moved along to get cutlery, she winked at me.

For the rest of the lunch hour I was in a daydream. I couldn't remember what I said or even who I served. All I thought about was the polar bear skull. It was strange for sure — and familiar — but why?

"Get yer head out of the clouds, girl. You're sloppin' soup all over the place, ya dropped the ladle into the pot twice, and now we're out of cutlery. Go get some more, ya silly thing."

Boy, Bertha was awful snippy. It wasn't as if she was super-focused herself. That morning, after we made the quiche, she'd put them in the oven and gone off to make a phone call. I was the one who'd noticed the temperature wasn't even on. When I took them out so I could preheat the oven, Bertha had snapped at me. "But the oven wasn't on — and I know you weren't planning to solar cook them," I'd snapped back.

"Oh, well, then, fine," she'd said without so much as a thank-you. Then she'd begun preparing the chowder and gotten distracted — burned the milk and had to start over again. "Mind yer own business, girl. We need more grated cheese, and see if the chocolate cake has thawed. If it has, cut it into squares and put them onto a platter."

Bertha always acted like a drill sergeant — all grumpy and demanding. But that day she was worse than usual, and on top of that, forgetful. So now, when I was a little distracted, she'd made a supreme case out of it.

"Tomorrow's the last day fer field school. That means tonight's supper has to be extra-special. I was tinking about a shepherd's pie with lots of those lovely mashed potatoes we made together. And then a nice tossed salad, fresh dinner rolls, and some of my famous mushy peas," Bertha said after everyone was gone and we were cleaning up.

"Mushy peas? I've made those — just cook them to death, and voila, mushy peas."

Bertha chuckled for the first time that day. "That's not what mushy peas are, silly. First thing, ya don't cook 'em in a pot — ya fry 'em in a pan."

"Okay, mushy peas and shepherd's pie," I said. This time the potatoes wouldn't include bits of stuff off the floor. "So what about dessert?"

"Well, I was tinkin' of cheesecake with caramel drizzled over the top, baked until the caramel's a teensy bit crackled. It's my husband's favourite." Bertha's eyes suddenly welled up as if she were going to cry. "Oh, darn, something's got in me eye. I need a tissue." She left the kitchen quickly, and when she came back her eyes were red and puffy. "I need a little time to organize things, Princess. Ya run along and find something to do. But be back at three or I'll —"

"I know, I know, you'll clobber me," I said before she had a chance.

"Right! I'll clobber ya."

I went back to the tent and flopped down on my bed. Finally, I had time to think about Eddy's news. Something kept niggling at the back of my mind. I reached under my cot, pulled out my sketchpad, and opened it to the pictures I'd drawn the day I'd gone to the cave. I wasn't the artist type, but the sketches were pretty good. I'd forgotten how much detail I'd included — like how I'd drawn the rock cairn from two different angles. I had to let Eddy see these, I thought.

I studied the pictographs carefully. As I examined them, an idea struck me. The large animal standing over the human might just have been a bear. And the people with the pointy chins — could they be Vikings?

I jumped off my bed, grabbed my sketchbook, and took off for the Viking settlement. When I arrived, I went straight to the forge to see Niko. As I waited for him to finish with the visitors, I had to pinch myself to keep from interrupting. When they finally moved on, I practically jumped onto his lap. "Niko, I have something I need to talk with you about. It has to do with the cave Louise found."

"Well, tell me, girl, what's on yer mind?"

I sat next to him and told him everything Eddy had said about the skull and the arrowheads. Then I opened my sketchbook.

"What have ya there?" he asked.

"These are drawings I made when I was in the cave. They're pictographs on the walls, and this is the rock cairn that was inside."

"Ya say 'was inside'? Isn't it there anymore?"

"No, they excavated it. Well, first I knocked it over. But then they removed all the rocks and found an animal skull buried underneath."

"Ya don't say."

"Yah, and they even brought in an expert — a zoo-archaeologist. She said it was a polar bear skull. What makes it even more interesting are the arrowheads." I told him about how they were made of iron and how they had pierced the bear's skull in different places and that lots more were found in the cairn burial. "The other day you told me the story of Sigrid the Brave. Didn't you say it was a bear that killed her?"

"I did, indeed."

"Good, now what kind of bear? Do you know?"

"Indeed I do. It says right in the saga it was a great white bear. I imagine the author was referrin' to a polar bear."

"And the bear was killed by a stream of arrows shot from the forest, right?" I said.

"Right."

I pointed to the pictograph with the large animal and two human figures. "So this is what I'm thinking. This pictograph might be of the battle between Sigrid and the polar bear. And if I'm right, it means the Beothuk were there — watching."

"Very good deductive reasonin'. I tink you're right. They saw the whole thing. I'm sure they were always watchin'. The Norsemen came to the same conclusion when they found the bear's body and realized the arrows were iron-tipped. Since they hadn't traded them, it meant the Beothuk must have entered the settlement at night, taken the leftover slag from the forge, and made their own arrow tips. The Vikings then realized how vulnerable they were and the danger the Beothuk posed to them."

I sat still, taking in all the facts. This was huge. If I was right — that the pictographs were a record of that day and they were an actual visual record of the event — it confirmed the *Saga of Erik the Red* and the story of Sigrid the Brave. It also meant the skull in the cave was from the bear that killed Sigrid. "Niko, when you spoke to the field school last week, did you tell them about Sigrid?"

"No. They were only interested in hearin' about the *Saga of the Greenlanders*, the one that highlights the adventures of Leif Eriksson. They weren't interested in Thorfinn Karlsefni."

"That means they know nothing about Sigrid or how she died. They have no idea of the connection of the bear's skull to her and the Norsemen who came here." I folded up my sketchbook. "I've got to go and find my friend, Eddy. She needs to hear about this. Thanks, Niko."

"It sounds like you're the one to be tanked, young lady. Ya connected the dots. Let me know how the experts take the news."

Racing out of the sod house, I headed up the hill toward the field school, excited about telling Eddy what I'd discovered. When I found some of the students working on an excavation pit, I asked them if they'd seen Eddy.

"Look, you're not supposed to be here," said Taylor.

"But it's really important that I talk to her. Do you know where she is?" I pleaded. No one answered. Then I looked at Maile — she was signalling me by pointing her nose toward the visitor centre. I gave her a tiny nod and took off up the trail.

When I reached the wooden stairs, I took them two at a time. Out of breath, I burst into the centre. There were a few tourists peering at the glass cases containing Viking artifacts from the site. I took a moment to imagine the bear's skull inside a similar glass case and tourists reading about how it was found by two young girls and about the story of Sigrid and — "Get a grip, Peggy," I said aloud. Right, I had something important to do.

I ran down the hall to the lecture rooms, expecting Eddy to be there. But when I burst through the door I nearly collided with Professor Brant. "What a cow, Maile!" I growled under my breath.

"You!" Professor Brant demanded. "What are you doing here?"

I definitely got the feeling I wasn't welcome.

"Well? What do you want?"

"I … I was just looking for Eddy. Is she here?"

"Do you see her here? And even if she was, you're not to distract her from her work. Didn't I make myself clear to you the other day?"

"Yes. And I wouldn't have come except I've discovered something important about the cave site." I turned to leave, trying to think where I should look next.

"If you have information, I'm the lead archaeologist around here. You can tell me."

I didn't want to share with Mister Snotty Pants. He gave me the willies, and besides, I wanted Eddy to be the first to know.

"Well, what is it? I haven't got all day."

This guy definitely didn't like me. Maybe he'd feel different once he knew how I'd figured out the connection of the bear skull to the Norse girl. It might just be the thing that would make him warm up to me. Then I could get Louise and me back inside the cave.

"I know what the pictographs are about and how they're connected to the bear skull and the death of a Norse girl named Sigrid," I said boldly.

"It's no secret the Beothuk killed the bear."

"Yes, but why did they kill it? And why did they paint those pictures on the cave wall? And what do they mean? I know the answers to all those questions."

"You do, do you? Then you'd better sit down and tell me what you know."

I sat next to him and told him the story of Sigrid the Brave and her uncle, Thorfinn Karlsefni. I told him everything I'd learned from Niko about the *Saga of Erik the Red*. Then I opened my sketchbook and showed him my drawings. "You see these pictographs here? They're telling about the day Sigrid fought the bear. It shows that the Beothuk tried to stop it from killing her, but they were too late. In the saga it says the Norsemen returned to Greenland soon after her death. The cave, the paintings, the burial of the bear skull — all of it might have been their way of acknowledging their great fortune that the foreigners were gone and they finally had their land back."

Professor Brant sat quietly, contemplating my story. Then his face broke into a large, creepy smile. He was so pleased that he asked if he could have my sketchbook to show the others.

"Sure. I was going to give it to Eddy, anyway, but I guess I can let you have it for a while," I told him.

"All right, then. You run along. Bertha must need you in the kitchen," the professor said in a sort of charming voice that was a little on the sinister side.

I glanced at the clock on the wall. Crap! It was already three-thirty.

As I ran back to the cook tent, I hoped Bertha wasn't going to be too mad. Now that I'd shared my discovery with Professor Brant, perhaps he wouldn't be so mad at me anymore. Maybe Bertha would be pleased, too, and not be so hard on me. In fact, after today I'd bet I was on everyone's good side — or at least would soon be.

When I arrived, I tugged open the door and a black cloud oozed out from the kitchen. "Bertha," I gasped, coughing. I could see flames shooting out from under a pot on the stove, as if it had boiled over. "Bertha! Fire!" I ran to the sink and filled a container with water. Just as I was about to throw it onto the flames, Bertha came in.

"Stop!" she yelled. "Never throw water on a grease fire." She turned the stove off and slapped a lid on the pot of oil, then grabbed the box of baking soda and poured it over the flames. A few moments later the flames had shrivelled and finally gone out. The danger was over.

I let out a big sigh. "That was close." When Bertha didn't acknowledge what I'd said, I turned and saw that she was wincing with pain. "Are you burned? Is it your hands?" Without saying anything she staggered to the sink and held her hands under the cold water. Already the skin was bright red, and there were blisters. "Bertha, should I call the ambulance? Do you need a doctor?"

"No," she groaned. "Just get me the medical kit." She continued to wince from the pain, and I was afraid she needed more than a few bandages. "Peggy, you'll have to cleanse the skin and then apply bandages to my hands." I guess I must have looked doubtful that I could do all of that. "Don't worry. I'll tell ya what to do."

After all the DVDs of *ER* Mom had made me watch with her, I should have been used to icky stuff, but I wasn't. Old bones — fine. Blood and icky stuff — not so much. While I disinfected Bertha's burns, I breathed deeply to keep from upchucking.

When her hands were bandaged, we both sat silently. I looked at the clock. Dinner was supposed to be served in less than two hours. But the potatoes weren't peeled or cooked, the mushy peas and cheesecake were covered in baking soda, and the entire place was filled with the awful smell of smoke. And Bertha, with her injured hands, wasn't going to be much help.

I was used to Bertha always being tough and scary, so I was surprised when I noticed tears trickling down her face. "This is all my fault," she said. "What have I told ya over and over about kitchen fires? If I hadn't been so worried about my hubby, this never would've happened."

"Your husband? What happened to him?"

She sniffled and wiped her nose. "He's gone up to the Yukon, drillin' fer oil. But he's not a spring chicken anymore and that's hard work. He'll be far from home fer months. I don't want him to do it, but we have no choice. We're strapped fer money, and the girls ... they need our help."

I knew what it was like to be on a tight budget. After Dad died, my mom was always trying to make ends meet. It was one of the reasons we'd moved in with Aunt Margaret.

"And now I've gone and made a real mess of the dinner. What am I goin' to do? Professor Brant's goin' to be mad as a hornet, and I've nothin' to serve."

"Well, look on the bright side, at least you don't have to be afraid of getting fired," I kidded. "You know ... since field school is finished after tomorrow, anyhow." She wasn't seeing the humour. I looked around the room for something to salvage. "This hamburger looks good. And you mixed in fried onions, too. There must be something we can make with this." Suddenly, a light bulb went on in my brain and I remembered the cookbook Aunt Margaret had stuck in my bag as I was leaving home. "I'll be back in a minute," I told Bertha.

Dashing to my tent, I rummaged under a pile of dirty clothes and found my backpack. When I pulled out the cookbook, my Great-Aunt B's Best Chili in the World recipe fell out almost like magic. I never imagined it was something I'd ever use — not in a million years.

"I know what we're having for dinner," I announced when I ran back into the kitchen. "And we'll use the barbecue and make it a cookout picnic." Surprisingly, Bertha didn't have a thing to say.

I read off the ingredients, and she directed me to the shelves where I could find everything. As fast as I could, into the biggest pot I could find, I poured diced tomatoes, tomato sauce, kidney beans, and chili powder, then threw in the chopped celery and green peppers meant for the salad. Finally, I added the cooked hamburger meat.

Outside, the gas barbecue was ready, and I lugged the pot of chili out and put it on the grill. "Bertha, are you able to stir?"

"Yah, I'll manage. Get out the frozen buns and we'll thaw them with the heat of the barbecue."

"Right. Then after that I'm going to drag chairs and tables out onto the grass." Man, I'd never worked so hard or so fast, but the clock was ticking even faster.

"Bertha, what are we going to have for dessert? There's no time to make anything. How about we serve ice cream?"

"That'll do. And we can throw on some sweetened bakeapples, too. There's a bowl of them in the fridge."

Good. We had a main course and a dessert. We were going to get through this thing. As I raced off to get the cutlery and serving utensils, Bertha called me back.

"I just want to say one thing, Princess. Tanks. Things would've been much worse if ya hadn't been here." Bertha got teary again. "You're a good girl, Peggy. A little odd and wayward at times, but all the same, a good girl."

"Sorry about your hands, Bertha."

"Ach, I'm a tough cookie. Okay, enough of this sweet talk. Get goin', Princess."

I stood guard at the door to the dining tent as people started to arrive and directed them to the picnic tables instead. Bertha covered her hands with oven mitts so no one could tell she'd burned them. What a relief — our cookout was a big success and seemed to lend itself to celebrating the end of a successful field school. With the air of festivity, no one even knew about the kitchen fire. Especially Professor Brant, who was in a particularly good mood. I was sure my news had something to do with it.

"Great chili, and I love the cookout idea. Please pay my compliments to the chef," Eddy said after supper.

"Actually, if you like the chili," I boasted shamelessly, "you can thank me for it. It's my great-aunt's recipe. Though Bertha helped some."

"You made the chili? The girl who said she never wanted to learn to cook properly?"

"Yah, I know. But I could hardly help it — given I've been a prisoner in this kitchen for most of the time I've been here."

"I'm sorry about that, Peggy. I thought things would be different. For starters, I never imagined the job of cook's help was so demanding."

"I'm just glad I got through it, and I did learn lots about the Vikings. And even though I did get into some trouble over the cave, I think it's great how things all turned out in the end."

"Turned out in the end?" asked Eddy.

"Well, you know, like how I discovered that the cave paintings are telling the story of Sigrid the Brave's battle with the bear and how the burial of the skull was like some ritualistic burial. Didn't Professor Brant tell you about it?"

"Yes, he did tell me. But, Peggy, I find it odd that you say we have you to thank for putting all the pieces together about the cave when, in fact, Professor Brant was the one to put it all together."

I was stunned. Eddy didn't believe me. "No. I went to see him earlier today. I took him my sketchbook and showed him how the details on the cave walls matched Sigrid the Brave's story. I'm the one who figured it out, Eddy. You can ask Niko, the storyteller."

"We'll have to talk about this more later, Peggy. I've got to go now. There's to be some speeches and acknowledgements."

As she walked away, I felt as if all the life had been sucked out of me. I knew Professor Brant was a jerk, but Eddy was my friend. How could she not believe me?

During all the speeches, Bertha called me over. "Tanks, Princess. No one has a clue about what happened. Ya sure saved my bacon."

"No problem." I noticed Bertha's face was red and that she had beads of perspiration all over her forehead. "Bertha, you don't look so good. Maybe you should have your hands looked at."

"Maybe I will, but we need to get this place cleaned up first."

"I can handle the cleanup. You go and lie down." It took a lot of insisting, but Bertha finally agreed to have a rest.

After hauling bins of dirty dishes into the kitchen, I loaded the dishwasher, then made several trips back and forth to get more dishes. As I did, I watched various students and professors get up and thank this person and that person for being helpful, for being an inspiration, and for teaching them the skills of excavation. Eddy's name came up several times, along with Professor Brant's. I got angry watching him gloat as adoring students praised him over and over. They all thought he'd solved the mystery about the cave. Even Eddy thought it was him.

Eventually, everyone cleared off and headed for the visitor centre for the last evening lecture. It took a long time to finish cleaning up, and when I was done, I took out Bertha's menu plan to see what she had in mind for breakfast.

"You need any help?" asked a voice from behind. I turned to see Robbie standing at the kitchen door. "I noticed that Bertha left you on your own. That's a lot of dishes and pots and things."

"Bertha wasn't feeling well. She went to rest for a while. But I'm finished now." I was hoping that would be it, but she didn't move.

"Exciting news about the cave, eh?"

I wasn't sure what to say. Every time Robbie started a conversation with me, it usually ended with sarcastic remarks. I didn't want to walk into her trap. "What news?"

"Oh, just how Professor Brant won a bid that will give him additional funds toward the excavation here at L'Anse aux Meadows. It'll probably continue through the fall. And now he knows the pictographs and the

saga of Sigrid the Brave are connected. It's really exciting, don't you think?"

I didn't know what to make of the conversation we
were having. Robbie appeared friendly, but I wasn't buying it. "Yah, exciting." I hung up my apron and moved to
the door. "Sorry, but I've got to see how Bertha is doing."

"Sure. See you in the morning. What's for breakfast?"

"Bertha planned for breakfast burritos, muffins, and
yogourt."

"Sounds great. I'll look forward to it. Well, good
night then." She turned and left.

I stood there wondering what that was all about.
What was she up to?

When I went to the tent, Bertha was sound asleep.
I didn't want to wake her, so I just crawled into my cot.
I was so tired I didn't even bother to undress. It didn't
take long before I was fast asleep, too.

*"It is as certain as I am sitting here talking to you that one
day the gods are doomed to perish. Odin even foretold
it himself," Sigrid tells Gunnar and the others who have
gathered around the hearth. "In that day the mountains
will shake and the ground will tremble. And Skoll, the
monstrous wolf, will leap upon the sun and gobble it
up. And the stars and sparks of Muspellheim will flicker
out and there will be complete darkness throughout all
of Midgard."*

*Gunnar shifts uncomfortably on the bench. "My
father will want me to come and help," he tells his cousin.*

*"You're not scared, are you?" teases Sigrid. "Don't you
want to hear how Fenris-wolf is going to break free from*

his prison and how he'll join with all the frost and storm giants to battle Odin, Thor, and the other gods?"

"I'm not scared. Besides, I've heard the story before. I just don't care to hear it again right now," Gunnar tells his older cousin.

"Fine, just as long as you understand that the end will come." Sigrid is pleased that Gunnar's eyes are as big as onions.

"Don't forget the rest of the story," butts in Aunt Gudrid. "Out of the ruins of old Asgard a new world will arise and the younger gods who don't perish and all mankind will rise up and build a new home where all will live in peace."

Sigrid stands and thrusts the stick she is using to poke the fire into the air. "Yes, but only the brave will live in such a place — only those who aren't afraid to battle with evil."

"Sigrid, did you do what I asked you to do?" Aunt Gudrid says to change the subject.

"Not yet," she answers. "I'm in the middle of telling a story."

"You cheeky girl. Get on with it. I told you I need more firewood, and I need it now. We're drying fish today."

Sigrid storms to the door and snatches up the basket.

"Snorri, go with your cousin," Gudrid tells the little boy.

Sigrid growls and takes her cousin's hand. "Keep up," she says briskly, and he toddles after her as fast as he can.

Aunt Gudrid watches her children leave. Though Sigrid dislikes babysitting, she will never let anything happen to Snorri, especially since the incident in the forest. When they are out of sight, she returns to preparing the fire moss. It really is the worst of all the jobs.

"Where are the children?" Thorfinn asks when he comes in for his morning meal.

"I've sent them off to gather firewood. If I don't keep that girl busy, she'll get into trouble," she tells him. "When she returns, I'm going to put her to work spinning yarn. Like it or not, she's got to get used to women's work."

Thorfinn sits beside the hearth. "Gudrid, I've been thinking about the match we made with Bjorni. I'm not so sure now it's a good one."

"I've been thinking the same thing. Poor man. He'd provide well for Sigrid, but I don't think he'll know how to handle one so defiant and lively as that girl. He needs a wife who appreciates security over freedom. And, besides, he's so old."

"He's younger than I," Thorfinn objects.

His wife laughs. "Yes, but he's still too old for Sigrid."

The couple fall into silence, and soon the demands of preparing for the journey home occupy their thoughts. When a good deal of time has passed and Sigrid has not returned with the necessary supply of wood, Gudrid grows annoyed. "That girl, all I asked her to do was gather some firewood and then come right back. I should have sent Gunnar instead. I'll have to see where she's gotten to."

Gudrid does not really mind the chance to go outside — she needs the fresh air. But when she reaches the edge of the settlement she does not see the children. Instead she sees the form of a great white bear rising on its hind legs and looking very angry.

"Thorfinn Karlsefni!" she screams. "Come quickly!"

When her husband hears her cries, he comes at once. "The children, where are they?" he asks when he sees the danger.

"I don't know. I'll look for them." Gudrid returns a few minutes later, her face as white as snow. "They haven't returned to the settlement," she whimpers.

"Get your weapons, men," commands Thorfinn to the crowd that has gathered. "Arrows, spears, axes!"

While the men head off to fetch their weapons, Thorfinn races toward the meadow. If he has to, he will fight with only his fists and wit. When he realizes he is too far, he yells to distract the creature. But the bear is focused on something else, and it roars and bares its teeth. Thorfinn thinks there is a streak of red seeping down its chest as it growls at something small and crumpled on the ground. Then Thorfinn realizes what it is.

"Sigrid!" he cries. "Oh, gods of Asgard, do something!" As if his prayer is heard, a stream of arrows falls from the sky and rains down on the bear. The great animal lets out a frightening bellow and drops heavily in a heap, blood pouring from its wounds.

When Thorfinn reaches the scene minutes later, the bear is still and lifeless. A short way off his son is resting his tiny head on Sigrid's chest. The boy's cheeks are stained with tears. Thorfinn drops to the ground beside them both. He gently shakes Sigrid, but it is clear her spirit is gone. When he tries to pry Snorri away, the boy refuses to let go of Sigrid's tunic.

Finally, Snorri climbs onto his father's lap. That is when Thorfinn glances at the lifeless, bloodstained heap and the arrows protruding from the bear's body. How could that be? he wonders. Where did they come from? Then he notices Sigrid's silver cloak pin stuck in the animal's neck.

"Oh, Sigrid," Thorfinn wails. "Brave young warrior. Go in peace. You have fought well." Thorfinn wipes his eyes, buries his head in his hands, and thinks back to the day he taught her to defend herself. He told her then, "If *you're going to kill, then drive the sword in like you mean it." He saw then that she enjoyed the sport but did not possess the ruthlessness to actually kill another.*

"But she tried, Snorri, and she did it to protect you. Rest in peace, my dear girl."

It was a long night for Bertha and me. She was restless from the pain in her hands. And I couldn't sleep because I had all the events of the day stomping around in my head. The worst part was finally doing something right, but no one knew about it. I wouldn't have minded so much if at least Eddy believed me.

CHAPTER TEN

"You're a good girl, Princess. If ya ever want a reference, just call me. And if ya ever want to be my cook's help again, well, don't," joked Bertha. Her throaty cackle sounded like the blender when I overfilled it. At least it meant she was in a decent mood that morning.

"How do your hands feel?" I asked.

"They hurt like hell, but they're better, tanks."

Bertha's hands may have been mending, but she still couldn't do much. She made the orange juice, poured yogourt into cups, and mixed the fruit salad. I did the rest — scrambled five dozen eggs, prepared all the fixings and condiments, cut up all the fruit, made the coffee, and set up the dining hall. If this had happened two weeks ago, we'd have been in trouble. But at least now I had a handle on making scrambled eggs. Though Bertha did catch me about to add too much chili powder again.

"The recipe says a couple of teaspoons, Princess, not a couple of tablespoons. Ya can read, can't ya?"

It was funny how that kind of stuff used to get under my skin, but now I just shrugged it off.

When everyone arrived, breakfast was piping hot and ready to go. Bertha stayed in the kitchen to avoid questions about her hands, and I served. I was anxious to see how people liked my cooking. Even though I'd never admit it to Aunt Margaret, I was kind of proud of the fact that I'd improved. I think I was even starting to like cooking.

"Hi, Eddy," I said when she got to the front of the line. "Do you want your breakfast burrito with or without beans?"

"With beans, thank you."

I spread a scoop of beans on a tortilla and added the scrambled eggs and salsa, then rolled it all up. "Here you go." I was getting better at rolling the tortilla so all the stuff didn't squish out.

"Looks good," she said. "Ah, Peggy, I'm sorry about last night — for not believing what you told me." I knew Eddy meant what she'd said by the way her eyes were all soft.

"I guess I can understand why you didn't believe me. I mean, I have bungled a lot of things since coming here. So why did you change your mind?"

"Because of me." I looked over and there was Robbie smiling. "I told her what really happened." I must have seemed confused. "You see, I was out in the hall when you were talking to Professor Brant yesterday. I heard the whole thing — like how you discovered the connection between the saga and the cave paintings. Later, during our lecture, he told everyone about it, only he left out the part about you being the one to put the pictographs and the bear skull together with the Norse girl. Everyone assumed he was the one who figured it all out. When he did nothing to correct their misperception, I got really peeved. I mean, who does something like that? Taking advantage of a little kid is just repugnant. Anyway, that's why I went to see Professor McKay this morning."

I was a little offended by the "little kid" part, but otherwise I was pleased and grateful to her. "Thanks, Robbie."

"That's okay, kid. I knew Professor McKay would know I wasn't making it up — seeing how we haven't exactly been best of friends. Besides, there's nothing I hate more than an arrogant liar."

I suddenly recalled some of the boastful things I'd said when I first arrived at L'Anse aux Meadows, and felt blood rush to my cheeks. At least I hadn't lied. "Well, it doesn't really matter as long as you guys know," I said.

"So what, now all of sudden you're humble after weeks of showing off?" Robbie said. "I don't think so." My cheeks were really on fire now. "Credit should be given where it's due."

"I agree," said Eddy. "It was excellent deductive reasoning, and because of you we're able to understand how these events are connected. It will move our study along much faster."

"Someone would have figured it out sooner or later," I offered.

"You're probably right, but all the same, you did some good work here," Robbie said. "So now all we need to do is figure out how to turn this to your advantage. I mean, you do want to get back into that cave, don't you?"

"Do I ever," I blurted.

"Well, just follow my lead."

I wasn't sure what she meant but decided to wait and see what happened. When everyone was finished their meal, Robbie started tapping her fork on her coffee cup and continued tinkling until everyone stopped talking and turned their attention to her. Then she stood up.

"I know last night we acknowledged the professors for all they've done to make this a great field school," Robbie said. I noticed Professor Brant's chest puff out as if he was sure she was referring to him. "But I just want to take this opportunity to thank some other people. First, I want to make a toast to Bertha for being the best camp cook." Everyone cheered and applauded enthusiastically. "Come out here, Bertha." At first she refused, but when everyone began banging their cups on the table and saying, "Bertha, Bertha, Bertha," she finally wrapped her hands inside a tea towel and came out to the dining hall.

"Tanks, it was my pleasure. You're a nice bunch of people," she said modestly. It was amusing to see big Bertha appear so demure. Not exactly the way I'd come to know her.

Then Robbie continued. "And I think we should acknowledge the cook's help. She's been notorious for being a preteen know-it-all —" my face suddenly melted like hot wax "— but she made a lot of progress both in and out of the kitchen." The applause for me was hardly audible. "And though she's prone to burning toast and her muffins are terrible —" Robbie's speech was starting to sound more like a roast rather than an acknowledgement "— she's got a real talent for figuring out puzzles. Isn't that right, Professor Brant?" Everyone looked at the professor, who shrugged as if he were waiting for the punch line to a joke. "Peggy, why don't you tell us how you realized the cave paintings depicted an event in one of the Norse sagas?"

I stood up, aware that all eyes were on me. I'd been trying to get these people to take notice of me ever since

I'd arrived, and now that they were I was wishing they'd stop. Awkwardly, I began to explain how my interest in shield maidens led me to Niko, the saga expert, to learn more about them. "He told me the story of a girl who came here more than a thousand years ago. Her name was Sigrid Thorbjornsdottir. She was brave and strong and wanted one day to be a warrior — not a common thing for females at the time. Only her first battle turned out to be her last when she met with an angry and hungry polar bear." I then explained how I realized that the cave paintings appeared to be telling a similar event and when I showed my sketches to Niko he agreed with me. When I finished my story, there was a long silence.

Finally, Robbie said, "That's great, Peggy. And what's really neat is how instead of keeping all this valuable information to yourself, you went straight to Professor Brant with it and told him all about it. Isn't that right, Professor?"

Professor Brant had beads of sweat on his forehead, and though he was smiling, it was one of those "I'm a dork" smiles. "Well, of course," he admitted, "the girl helped … somewhat."

"The girl's name is Peggy," Eddy said. "And I'd say she moved things along considerably. And though she did make some serious mistakes, it would be a well-deserved reward if she and her friend, Louise — who I should add was responsible for finding the cave — were given permission to spend some time there. I, for one, think we could use their help."

The professor didn't object. I think he was just glad nothing else was said. So, later that day, Louise and I joined Eddy in the cave. When I entered, I had goose bumps all up and down my arms and back. The first thing I wanted to see was the exposed bear skull. It was huge, and its jaw was opened wide to bare its dangerous teeth. I got a creepy image in my head of the day the bear had killed Sigrid. I figured even Thor couldn't have brought down a bear so big without the help of the Beothuk.

I was envious when Eddy told me she was staying for another week to finish excavating the skull and then arrange for protection of the site, which for now was called Three Girls Cave — after Louise, me, and Sigrid. What was worse, Louise was going to help her.

"Don't worry, Peggy. You're still my right-hand girl."

Even if I was jealous, I knew Louise deserved this chance.

As Eddy and Louise examined the bear skull closer, I took the flashlight and walked around the cave. Now that I knew what had happened, all the pictographs made perfect sense. There was the Viking ship arriving with the pointy-chinned Norsemen. Next were several scenes of hunting, trading, and fighting. Near the end was the scene with the bear and Sigrid's death.

"Eddy, I didn't notice this before," I said, pointing to a small pictograph just before the departing ship. She and Louise joined me, and we all studied it together. "It looks like a fire down by the beach — and something burning in the middle."

"It is done. Her body is washed and prepared for cremation," Gudrid says softly. Her grief is great, yet she does not have one tear left to shed. "Is the funeral pyre ready?"

"No," says Thorfinn. "We must gather more wood. The fire must be big enough to consume every part of her. Only then will her spirit be released and be free to journey to its rightful place."

They both stare at the neatly wrapped body lying on the table. Only Snorri, who plays alone on the floor, seems unaffected. Yet even he cried for her all last night.

"To die so young — it should never have happened," Gudrid murmurs.

"True, yet to die so bravely — it's how every warrior chooses to go."

"She was a girl, Thorfinn Karlsefni, not a warrior. You never should have encouraged her to think she was anything else. Maybe then she'd still be here with us today."

Thorfinn points to his son on the floor. "He's the reason she isn't here with us today. Because she had the heart of a warrior she fought to protect Snorri. Gudrid, can't you see? More than anything she wanted her life to have purpose, and nothing would have made her more proud than to end her life in battle defending someone she loved." Thorfinn pounds his chest to stop himself from shedding tears. "For this she will live out her days in Valhalla. Oh, Gudrid, can't you see? She would never have been a good wife or mother no matter how hard you tried to make her." His wife says nothing, for in her heart she knows he is right. "I only hope that I should go so bravely and not as an old man in my sleep."

Gudrid slumps onto the bench. "You and your grand ideas of dying with honour. I don't want to hear any more of it. The fault is mine. I was the one who sent her out there alone."

Gunnar enters the house and senses that he has come at an awkward moment. "Excuse me, Aunt and Uncle, they wish to place the body on the pyre now." Gunnar cannot lift his eyes to where the body rests. Sigrid's voice — heard only the day before — still rings in his ears. Now she is far away, and he will never see her again.

When Thorfinn gives the signal, Ellandar sets the pyre alight and almost instantly it bursts into flames. They watch as the glow of the fire lights the night sky. Then a watchman is set for every hour of the evening, ensuring the flames continue to burn bright and that they lick up every last ounce of Sigrid's body. As the smoke rises to the sky, it carries with it her spirit into Asgard.

The next morning, when the sun peeps over the horizon, there is nothing left but ashes. Before they cover them with soil and rocks, Gudrid kisses Sigrid's hammer-shaped amulet and places it on the remains. Thor's Mjolnir pendant was the only thing the girl had of her own mother's. Then Thorfinn places her cloak pin in the ashes, too — the one she used to stab the bear. "You may need such a thing where you are going, Sigrid." When the last of the ash is covered and the rocks placed over the grave, the community returns to the settlement.

"Now we'll wait the necessary seven days, and after the celebration of Sigrid's life, we'll set sail," Thorfinn tells his wife. "Despite all that's happened here, I'll miss this place and all its potential. But it's clear to me now that it will never be home to the Norsemen."

All that week the settlers work to complete their tasks. Some must gather, dry, and store sufficient food and water *for the journey. Others load furs and fell trees to lash to the sides of the knarrs.*

"Uncle, Uncle!" shouts Gunnar, arriving out of breath. "It's not there. It's gone."

"What are you talking about, boy?" Thorfinn asks. "What's gone?"

"The bear. The bear." No one asks what bear, for it is understood immediately what the boy is speaking about.

Thorfinn and others go with Gunnar to the scene of Sigrid's death. When they arrive, there is no sign of the bear's carcass. Thorfinn leans down and examines the ground carefully. "Someone has butchered the animal. Look here — you can see fragments of bone and scraps of fur."

"And the boulders here are covered in blood and flesh. They must have used this as a chopping block," adds Gunnar.

Thorfinn turns slowly, looks toward the forest, and has an eerie feeling of being watched. "Let's go. There's much to do."

No one speaks of the incident when they return to the settlement. It will only upset the others.

The day the men row the knarrs away from the shore the sun is high and the winds are strong. When they are a safe distance from the rocky shoreline, Thorfinn gives the order to set the sails. Soon each of the three ships picks up speed and the Norsemen head northward.

Thorfinn holds his son as they watch the settlement get smaller in the distance. Then Snorri becomes restless and reaches back to the land. "No leave Sig-id," he whimpers. "No leave Sig-id."

"Shhh, Snorri. Sigrid can't come. She's gone to Valhalla to be with the gods," says Thorfinn. He knows Snorri does not understand and holds him tight when the boy begins to cry.

I was hoping by the time I returned home Aunt Margaret would have finished painting the house. But no such luck.

"You have a choice, Peggy," said Aunt Margaret before I climbed the stairs for bed. "Tomorrow you can either paint or shop for new school clothes."

"Not much of a choice. I guess I'll have to pick painting."

Aunt Margaret smiled. "I thought so. But you know school's starting soon." Then she got all silly and excited. "And this is a special year — you're finally beginning junior high school. I loved high school. It's when I started wearing high heels, makeup … and got interested in boys!"

"Stop, already. You're making me ill," I complained.

Mom wrapped her arms around me and laughed. "Oh, Peggy. You're going to have to face it sooner or later — you're growing up."

When I finally reached my bedroom that night, I flopped onto my comfy bed. I'd been looking forward to having a good sleep, but on some weird level I knew I was going to miss waking in the night to the sounds of Bertha. I looked over to my dresser to her going-away present to me. It was one of those cheesy Viking helmets with horns. I totally loved it and had laughed when she gave it to me.

"Thanks for everything, Bertha. It's sure been a slice," I'd said the day I left.

"Maybe fer you," she'd kidded. "But like they say, if ya can't stand the heat, then get out of the kitchen."

The next morning when I woke it was still dark outside and the house was quiet. I figured the automatic alarm clock in my brain was still set on Newfoundland time. But once I was awake there was no going back to sleep. Besides, I was too used to getting up at the crack of dawn to the sounds of drill-sergeant Bertha.

I tiptoed down the stairs and into the kitchen. I was a little hungry and opened the fridge to see what there was to eat. In the past I would have seen nothing good. Now all I could see was endless potential.

Out came the milk, the eggs, the butter, and the cinnamon. A short while later the pan was sizzling and the air was filled with a delicious smell. When I was done, I stood back and admired the stack of French toast I'd made.

"Breakfast in bed?" Mom said when I delivered her French toast. "How sweet, honey. But it's so early."

"Yah, that's what Aunt Margaret said when I took her some, too. She thought my French toast was delicious," I boasted. "I told her, 'That's nothing — wait till you taste my chili.'"

AUTHOR'S NOTE

I learned a lot about the Viking Age while researching for this book. There are many popular but false impressions about these people. For instance, they never had horned helmets and the term *Viking* wasn't a synonym for Norsemen but rather an activity. To go on a Viking was to go exploring, trading, and yes, sometimes pillaging.

The Norse were amazing shipbuilders, explorers, artisans, and inventors. They originated in Denmark, Norway, and Sweden. The Viking Age was from about A.D. 700 to A.D. 1100. While Sigrid and various other characters are fictitious, Gudrid Thorbjornsdottir, Thorfinn Karlsefni, and their son, Snorri, were real people who travelled from Greenland to what is now called L'Anse aux Meadows around A.D. 1000. As far as we know, Snorri was the first European to be born in North America. They were fascinating people and are worth learning more about.

Another fact is the two versions of the Norse voyage to Vinland — *Saga of the Greenlanders* and *Saga of Erik the Red*. They have many similarities between them, but one alludes to Thorfinn Karlsefni as having more impact than the more popularly known Leif Eriksson. Which is true? The experts are still debating.

While L'Anse aux Meadows is the only place in North America, so far, where there is absolute evidence that the

Vikings sailed here, for some the butternut squash offers proof they travelled farther south. The butternut squash wasn't indigenous to Newfoundland, and since seeds from this vegetable were excavated at L'Anse aux Meadows, it at least raises the possibility that the Norse voyaged south and traded with the indigenous people there.

The term *skraeling* was used by the Norse and referred to the indigenous people of North America. Literally translated, it means "barbarian" or "foreigner." This is ironic, since it was the Norse who were the foreigners. Other Viking terms used in this novel are: *Thing* (a meeting of the clan leaders), *thrall* (a slave), *knarr* (Viking flat-styled sailing boat), *berserker* (warriors who fought in a near trance-like state), *mead* (wine), *fimmt* (the Viking five-day week), and *hnefatl* (a Viking board game similar in aspects to chess and checkers).

When I first started writing this book, I thought it was going to be just about the Vikings who came to Canada. But what I realized was it's impossible to isolate them from their interaction with the Beothuk. Now I see it's nearly impossible to write about most aspects of Canadian history without looking at the connection to the First Nations people. After all, they were here first!

SELECTED READING

Cadnum, Michael. *Raven of the Waves*. New York: Orchard Books, 2001.

Chisholm, Jane, and Struan Reid. *Who Were the Vikings?* New York: Usborne Publishing, second edition, 2002.

Picard, Barbara Leonie. *Tales of the Norse Gods*. Oxford: Oxford University Press, 2001.

Wallace, Birgitta. "Viking Farewell," *The Beaver: Canada's History Magazine*, January 2007.

IN THE SAME SERIES

Reading the Bones
A Peggy Henderson Adventure
Book 1

Due to circumstances beyond her control, twelve-year-old Peggy Henderson has to move to the quiet town of Crescent Beach, British Columbia, to live with her aunt and uncle. Without a father and separated from her mother, who's looking for work, Peggy feels her unhappiness increasing until the day she and her uncle start digging a pond in the backyard and she realizes the rock she's been trying to pry from the ground is really a human skull.

Peggy eventually learns that her home and the entire seaside town were built on top of a 5000-year-old Coast Salish fishing village. With the help of an elderly archaeologist, a woman named Eddy, Peggy comes to know the ancient storyteller buried in her yard in a way that few others can — by reading the bones.

As life with her aunt becomes more and more unbearable, Peggy looks to the old Salish man from the past for help and answers.

Broken Bones

A Peggy Henderson Adventure

Book 2

A vandalized burial in an abandoned pioneer cemetery brings twelve-year-old Peggy Henderson and her elderly archaeologist friend Eddy to Golden, British Columbia, to excavate. The town dates back to the 1880s when most of the citizens were tough and rowdy miners and railway workers who rarely died of old age. Since the wooden burial markers disintegrated long ago, Peggy and Eddy have no way of knowing the dead man's identity. But when Eddy discovers the vertebrae at the base of the skull are crushed, a sure sign the cause of death was hanging, they have their first clue.

Peggy's tendency to make quick judgments about others leads her to the conclusion that only bad people are hanged, so the man in the burial must have gotten what he deserved. Hoping to learn more about him that proves her beliefs, she is soon digging through dusty old newspapers at the small-town museum. It's there that Peggy learns that sometimes good people do bad things.

Bone Deep

A Peggy Henderson Adventure

Book 3

An expedition to investigate an old sunken ship teaches Peggy lessons about herself.

When archaeologists discover a two-hundred-year-old shipwreck, Peggy Henderson decides she'll do whatever it takes to take part in the expedition. But first she needs to convince her mom to let her go, and to pay for scuba diving lessons. To complicate matters even more, Peggy's Great Aunt Beatrix comes to stay, and she's bent on changing Peggy from a twelve-year-old adventure-seeking tomboy to a proper young lady. Help comes in the most unlikely of places when Peggy gets her hands on a copy of the captain's log from the doomed ship, which holds the key to navigating stormy relationships.